GIRLS CAN VLOG

Hashtag Hermione
Wipeout!

Emma Moss loves books, cats and YouTube. In that order – though it's a close call.

Books by Emma Moss

The Girls Can Vlog series

Lucy Locket: Online Disaster

Amazing Abby: Drama Queen

Hashtag Hermione: Wipeout!

MACMILLAN CHILDREN'S BOOKS

First published 2017 by Macmillan Children's Books
an imprint of Pan Macmillan
20 New Wharf Road, London N1 9RR
Associated companies throughout the world
www.panmacmillan.com

ISBN 978-1-5098-1740-5

Based on an original concept by Ingrid Selberg

1 3 5 7 9 8 6 4 2

A CIP catalogue record for this book is available from
the British Library.

Design by Lizzy Laczynska
Printed and bound by CPI Group (UK) Ltd, Croydon CR0 4YY

For all the awesome bookworms out there

Chapter One

Dear Diary,

So, yeah. Christmas was pretty weird. Voldemort-in-the-Forbidden-Forest weird. Aragog weird. It was just weird.

OK, maybe the holidays weren't THAT bad, but everything's changing really quickly and it's so confusing. Let's just say it will be a big relief to go back to school in a couple of days. Now that Mum and Dad have told me about the divorce, they aren't bothering to hide how much they *totally loathe* each other. I never really noticed before but I guess they were acting happy compared to how they act now. Or maybe I was just being thick . . .

Dad moved out to a hotel a few days ago and Mum is in a terrible mood and taking it out on Yours Truly. When it's only the two of us, she just wants to harp on about school and whether I'm being 'challenged' enough. Seriously! Just because I get good marks doesn't mean I need extra homework! She also insisted on me getting this really extreme haircut for no good reason – she decided I was too old for long hair and I was spending too much time styling it. As you know, Diary, I'm thirteen. THIRTEEN. Not thirty. It was totally random, but I didn't have the nerve to fight her on it and now I have this square Lego helmet haircut – just like Mum's – which I can't style at all. It's truly awful.

It gets worse . . . When Dad drops by to see me or pick up some more clothes, Mum sulks in the bathroom with the door locked until he's gone, having long baths and turning up the radio. She's using all my bath bombs – oh sure, help yourself, Mum! The other day she WhatsApped me from in there to see if he'd left yet. Honestly. I thought I was meant to be the immature teenager around here. I still don't really know what actually happened between them – maybe I never will. I guess

I don't want to know? It must have been something really bad . . .

Dad's been the opposite to Mum and acting really cheerful, which is almost worse because it's not like him at all and I can tell he's faking it. One silver lining: he gave me the amazing vlogging camera I'd asked for at Christmas – woohoo – and now he's started bringing me little girly gifts, like lipgloss and bubble bath. Since when did he know about that stuff? So bizarre.

I don't know whether I feel more angry than upset about them splitting up. Did they even bother to think about how it was going to ruin my life?! Ergh, I can't start crying again in case I wreck you, beautiful new Diary. (Granny Paw Paw sends me one every year, but you are especially gorgeous: bound in lavender leather with thick creamy paper.) The others still don't know about the divorce news, apart from Abby who is amazingly managing to keep it secret. I just don't feel like talking about it – apart from to you, obviously, Diary.

At least my friends are keeping me sane and the Girls Can Vlog channel is doing really well. Since RedVelvet appeared in our Christmas tag video we have nearly 5,000 subscribers – eek! It makes me nervous if I think about it for too long. I reckon our videos are getting better and better, though. My new camera has got me really inspired about making videos, so watch this space . . .

Oh! One other exciting thing to report – I spotted an online creative-writing competition for writers aged thirteen to sixteen. The prize is the most incredible thing ever – a place on a writers' workshop at YA Writing Con, where you get tutored by a real-life author. Obviously I won't win, but it can't hurt to try, hey? The theme is 'fairytale with a twist' and the story has to be a thousand words long. I'm tempted to do something about Rapunzel and her long golden locks – as you can probably tell I'm sort of obsessed with nice hair right now. Sob!

Speak to you soon – gotta run to a GCV meeting at Abby's. We're filming a New Year vlog and apparently Lucy is bringing a surprise guest???

Hermione x

Hermione rang the doorbell, pulling her yellow beanie down over her awful hair as far as it would go.

'Hey, H!' cried Abby as she let her in. Immediately Weenie, Abby's little cream pug, skittered across the floorboards towards her and started yapping excitedly. 'It's only Hermione, Weenie,' said Abby. 'You know Hermione. She's had a new haircut, that's all – remember I showed you on Instagram?'

The pug stopped in his tracks and stared intently at Abby, almost as if he could understand every word.

'You show Weenie your Instagram?' asked Hermione, raising an eyebrow.

'Well, he does star in half my photos, so it's only fair that he gets to have a look,' giggled Abby. 'He loves my account! Anyway, how are you? How is . . . everything at home? Love your haircut, by the way. I know you hate it, but it makes your hair look so thick and shiny – not like my weedy wisps . . . And you're wearing those earrings we gave you! They look cool.'

Hermione knew Abby was just trying to make her feel

better – her hair was a disaster – so she gave Abby a quick hug. Then she glanced upstairs.

'It's OK, you're the first to arrive,' said Abby. 'Though I do think you're going to have to tell them soon.'

'I will, it's just . . . Lucy said she was bringing someone today, so it doesn't feel like the right time.' Hermione took off her duffle coat and scarf, and hung them on the coat rack. She went to pull off her beanie too, then decided to leave it on. 'So . . . it's pretty awkward at home still,' she started. 'In fact, it's vile. I'm just hanging out in my room a lot. Dad's been visiting but—'

The doorbell interrupted her and Abby smiled sympathetically. 'Tell me later,' she said as she went to open the door. 'OH MY GOD!' There was some very high-pitched squealing. 'Is this – Are you –? *Yes!* I recognize you! Hermione, come and see! This is hashtag *amazing*!'

Slightly unnerved by Abby's reaction and all the giggling on the doorstep, Hermione came to the door. There, standing next to a grinning Lucy, in a bright green coat and hot-pink scarf, was Morgan, Lucy's best friend

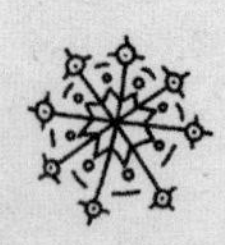

from America. Hermione had never met her, but she recognized her instantly from her YouTube channel, from her flowing red hair to her throaty laugh.

'Hey, you guys!' Morgan said warmly. 'Surprise!'

'Morgan s-surprised *me*, a couple of days ago!' said Lucy delightedly as they all hugged. 'Well, she organized it with m-my parents behind my b-back. We've been having such a great time. L-let's go inside – it's f-freezing out here.'

They bustled into the house and headed upstairs on Abby's command. Her room was still over-the-top Christmassy, with pink and gold tinsel draped from every surface, snowflake-shaped fairy lights twinkling behind the bed, and a mini Christmas tree laden with candy canes and tiny chocolate ornaments sitting on the corner of her dressing table. Of all the girls, Abby loved decorating the most – the more glitter and sparkle the better – and it was the perfect room for filming (although privately Hermione didn't know how Abby could put up with that level of sparkle twenty-four seven).

'It's so nice to meet you, Morgan,' said Hermione tentatively as Morgan looked around the room, squealing with admiration over Abby's things. She knew that Morgan was Lucy's best friend in the world, and even though she wasn't jealous (she didn't think) she felt kind of shy around her. 'How come you're in the UK?'

Morgan sat down on the bed, still holding one of Abby's fluffy jumpers that she'd pulled from her wardrobe. 'So, basically, guys, my parents were planning to come to my cousin's wedding – he's marrying an English girl this weekend – and they worked out the venue was only a couple of hours' drive away from Luce's place. So because I have been missing her SO MUCH—'

Lucy sat down beside her and gave her a hug. 'S-same here!'

'. . . we decided I could come too, and sneak in a surprise visit. Because why not? Life's way too short not to catch up with your bestie. Besides –' Morgan looked around at them all – 'I was dying to meet the

whole Girls Can Vlog team in real life, and maybe –' she gave Lucy a coy look – 'film a little guest appearance with them?'

'Of course!' yelled Abby, grabbing some gold tinsel and draping it round Morgan's neck. 'We've been dying to collab with you forever! After all, you're the one who got Lucy into vlogging – so our whole channel started up because of you.' Morgan had given Lucy her first camera as a goodbye present when she'd moved away from America, and Lucy hadn't looked back since.

'Abby's right,' said Hermione, getting her Girls Can Vlog notebook out of her bag. 'Plus, your videos are amazing – you've given us so many ideas. We're filming our New Year's resolutions today.'

The door opened.

'Knock-knock,' said Charlie. 'Jessie's here. Hi, guys. Hi . . . Abby.'

'Hey, Charlie,' said Abby. As Jessie noticed Morgan and flew over to hug her, Hermione watched Abby and Charlie carefully. Charlie was the best friend of Abby's older brother, Josh, and the boys filmed their own videos together on their channel Prankingstein. Over the last few months Abby and Charlie had become kind of close, but Hermione wasn't sure what was going on. Before she could draw any firm conclusions, Charlie had gone back downstairs.

'Is he gone already?' shouted Morgan. 'His videos with your brother are so funny, Abby.'

'They're hashtag *hilarious*,' agreed Lucy.

'And Abby and Charlie have great onscreen energy too, like when you filmed that prank on Josh together,' said Morgan. 'And did I detect some flirting?'

They all burst into giggles.

'Er . . .' squirmed Abby, for once lost for words, as everyone turned to watch her reaction. 'Can someone help me with this tripod?'

'Yeah, we should probably get filming,' said Hermione, diving in to rescue her friend. She felt a bit sorry for Abby – fun though Morgan was, subtlety wasn't her strong point.

'Yes!' cried Jessie, jumping on the bed. 'With our amazing guest star – how did I not know this girl was going to be here? Our first vlog of the year is going to be GOALS!'

VLOG 1

FADE IN: ABBY'S BEDROOM

ABBY, LUCY, JESSIE, HERMIONE and MORGAN all squeezed on to ABBY's bed. All wave at the camera. WEENIE is napping at ABBY's feet.

ABBY

Hi, everyone, Happy New Year from all of us at Girls Can Vlog! Hope you had an awesome Christmas.

LUCY

T-today we have a huge surprise for you: it's my best friend MORGAN over from the US of A! Everybody, m-meet Morgan!

(gestures to MORGAN)

MORGAN

Hi there! I'm sooo excited to be doing a collab with these girls today. New Year's resolutions, right, Hermione?

HERMIONE

Um, right!

MORGAN

I know, to make this a bit more fun, let's do the New Year's Q and A tag! I was tagged in this and I think I can remember the questions. OK, first up, what is your favourite memory of last year?

ABBY

(grinning)

Performing in *Grease* that first night . . . so worth it even though the rehearsals were a nightmare!

JESSIE

Mine was definitely filming with RedVelvet.

ABBY

Oh yeah, duh, that one for me too!

LUCY

Me three! And – I guess, my f-first date with Sam.

HERMIONE

Cute! I'd say all the Girls Can Vlog stuff has been amazing!

MORGAN

OK. Next question, what is something new

that you've tried this year?

LUCY, JESSIE and HERMIONE

Vlogging!

HERMIONE

(pulling a sad face)

. . . And a short haircut.

LUCY

And w-working on a farm, ha ha!

JESSIE

And doing a somersault on the beam!

ABBY

And achieving the perfect smoky eye!

WEENIE lets out a snore and they all giggle.

MORGAN

Finally, name one goal you have for the New Year.

ABBY

(grimacing)

I'd better say improving my grades . . . otherwise my 'something new' for next year will be 'repeating the year'.

MORGAN

(rolling her eyes)

Very hashtag *sensible* . . . now, how about something more fun? Such as, what are you going to do about your two boyfriends?

All the girls gasp and then start giggling. WEENIE wakes up, and looks around frantically at the noise.

MORGAN (CONTINUED)

OOH! Now you're blushing!

ABBY

(covering her face with her hands)

I AM NOT! Morgan, OMG, do you not have a filter?

JESSIE

(jumping up with excitement)

Well, now that Morgan's brought it up . . . what ARE you going to do? Charlie's clearly crazy about you, but you've got some unfinished business with Ben too.

ABBY

NOT the subject for a vlog! Moving on . . . and, Jessie, sit down!

MORGAN

Whatever – I recommend that Abby's second resolution is to sort out her love life! OK, next up, Hermione?

HERMIONE

More reading . . . always more reading! Last year I had a target of a book a week, but there are so many great books I need to read that I'd love to get to two a week. AND I am going to grow my hair back and no one is EVER going to make me cut it again! Maybe if I eat all the right vitamins and use some special oils and things, I can grow it back down to my shoulders at least by the end of the year.

LUCY

Hey, H, it d-doesn't look that bad! At least your hair is all straight and glossy!

JESSIE

(flipping her braids)

Yeah, you should try looking after mine!

MORGAN

OK, your turn, Lucy.

LUCY

Hmmm. Well, I'd r-r-really like to learn to ride properly—

MORGAN

(interrupts)

Ooh, that sounds sooo English! Prop-er-lee! Girl, you've gone all *Downton Abbey*.

LUCY

(swats Morgan)

Stop t-teasing! No, seriously. I want to be able to r-ride with Sam and eventually to be able to h-help out with the riding groups at the City Farm.

JESSIE

More gymnastics training for me! I want to get, like, really good. But also I've decided I really need to help my mum more at home – especially with my little brother Max.

MORGAN

But if you're going to be in the next Olympics you have to prioritize your training!

JESSIE

(laughing)

We'll see! What about you, then, Morgan? Your turn to spill . . .

MORGAN

I guess I need to stop biting my nails when I get stressed. I know, it's REALLY GROSS but I find it so hard to quit! If I do it, my mom is going to treat me to a salon manicure.

LUCY

G-good for you!

(she gives Morgan a hug)

MORGAN

Ooh, also, you guys should set some goals for your channel this

year. It's awesome that you're at five thousand
subscribers already!

ABBY

We're going to kill it! Let's aim for twenty thousand subscribers
by the end of the year.

HERMIONE pulls a surprised face.

ABBY (CONTINUED)

I know it's a lot, but we've got some amazing ideas
for videos. Another goal is for us to get to SummerTube
this year.

MORGAN

Great goal! That convention looks awesome. And now,
as a reward, I've got some treats for you from the USA.
Come and get 'em!

MORGAN picks up her bag and dumps a load of American

sweets on the bed: Tootsie Rolls, Reese's Cups, Christmas M&Ms. LUCY, HERMIONE, ABBY and JESSIE start fighting over the sweets and devouring them.

HERMIONE

(her mouth full)

Delicious! Let us know your goals for this year in the comments and we'll give a shout-out to the most inspiring ones in our next vlog. And don't forget to check out Morgan's channel – we've linked it down below.

They all wave goodbye. WEENIE has gone back to sleep.

FADE OUT.

Views: 1,201

Subscribers: 5,069

Comments:

So-Cal-Gal: Didn't know u were in England Morgan!! Any cute dudes?

MagicMorgan: In a word – yes! ☺

girlscanvlogfan: You'll ace the 20,000 this year ! 👍

queen_dakota: 20,000? LOL. You wish.

Sammylovesbooks: Soo impressed, Hermione – my resolution is 25 books a year.

SassySays: New subscriber here, currently binge-watching your videos! X

PrankingsteinCharlie: Good luck keeping your resolutions! Especially Abby 

(scroll down to see 13 more comments)

⏩

Chapter Two

'You were right, Luce, this place IS like Downton Abbey,' said Morgan in wonder as the girls reached their form room. Morgan had been allowed to shadow Lucy for the first day of term before heading back to the US with her parents. 'Hermione, it's lucky that you were here to show Lucy around when she started – it's sooo different to our school back home.'

Hermione smiled. That first term seemed like such a long time ago now. 'Lucy did great – apart from slipping in a giant puddle on her first day!'

'It *was* a pretty effective way of getting yourself noticed,' teased Jessie. 'By the entire class.'

'P-please don't remind me,' said Lucy, sitting down at her desk and sharing round some leftover Christmas cookies from a Tupperware container. 'And it wasn't even just our class – Dakota's v-video meant that the whole school w-witnessed my humiliation.'

'Oh yes, that was so EVIL of her,' cried Morgan. 'Where's this famous Dakota anyway – I've got a beef with her! And when are you gonna get your own back?' She glanced around curiously, taking stock of the other teenagers. 'Also, Abby, where is that cute dude Ben you were in *Grease* with? Lucy told me all about it. He's in your class, right? Do you like him as much as Charlie?'

Abby froze, her face a picture of embarrassment, and Hermione cringed in sympathy. Morgan had such a loud voice and Ben was only a few steps away from Lucy's desk. He was doing a good job of pretending not to listen, looking at something on his phone, but his cheeks had started to go bright red. As with Charlie, Hermione wasn't sure what was going on, but she knew that it was a sensitive topic – especially after Ben had snogged Dakota at the *Grease* after-party.

Not to Morgan, though, apparently. 'So, *are* Ben and Dakota together now?' she asked loudly. 'Abby, you're so awesome – I refuse to believe he picked her over you.' Hermione couldn't help but giggle as Abby, out of sheer desperation, lunged at Morgan and stuffed a cookie in her mouth.

'Students of Nine F, your attention please!' Miss Piercy called a few minutes later, over the back-to-school chatter. Hermione looked up from showing Lucy one of her favourite Christmas presents, a Harry Potter water bottle complete with the Hogwarts crest. 'Welcome back – and hello, Morgan, nice to have you with us today.'

'Thanks, it's great to be here!' said Morgan cheerily. 'Love that top, by the way!'

She's so confident, marvelled Hermione. *I could never talk to a teacher like that, especially one I'd never met before.* She caught Abby's eye and tried not to giggle.

'Well, thank you very much,' said the teacher, glancing

down at her turquoise and white polka dot jumper. 'Now, class, I'm sensing a new-term restlessness amongst you. I, too, am sorry that Christmas is over and that we're all stuck back in this classroom, but there is some news which may just take the edge off.' She smiled cryptically at her students.

'Homework has been discontinued?' shouted out Jessie.

'The canteen is being turned into a pizzeria?' said Eric. Ben cheered loudly in support of the idea and Hermione saw Abby steal a glance at him.

'Nearly as good as both of those,' said Miss Piercy. 'A half-term ski trip to France for Year Nines! It's a lovely resort in the Alps that the school goes to every year. A wonderful opportunity for those of you who are interested – all abilities welcome, and we can even cater for snowboarding lessons if enough of you are keen. A sign-up sheet is going up on the noticeboard.'

A ski trip? thought Hermione, looking at Lucy, their faces slowly lighting up together. That actually *was* exciting!

'I c-can't wait! This is g-going to be intense,' whispered Lucy, her stammer more pronounced with all the excitement. 'I love skiing! We should all go and v-v-vlog the whole trip!' Abby and Jessie gestured frantically at them from across the room – they obviously had the same idea. A Girls Can Vlog trip, the perfect thing to take their channel to the next level, like they'd discussed in their resolutions video.

'Guys, you should attach GoPro cameras to your helmets!' said Morgan enthusiastically, forgetting to lower her voice. 'They record the most amazing downhill footage and you can even monitor how fast you're going!'

But, as Miss Piercy continued to explain, Hermione's heart sank. Full parental approval was required and, with her mum in her current mood, she didn't rate her chances. Plus, the more she thought about it, the more she worried that she wasn't exactly cut out for racing down an icy slope . . . especially not with a vlogging camera in hand! But still – a trip away would be so much fun. She'd never been to France, and maybe it would give her inspiration for her competition entry. *Please, Mum . . .* she thought helplessly. *Just let this one thing go my way.*

Dear Diary,

So that was a complete and utter disaster! As Abby would say: hashtag fail!

I carefully picked a good moment to discuss the ski trip with Mum: during dinner, after I'd told her about the writing competition. She warned me not to get my hopes up, but I could tell she was happy about me entering. So then, as I brought our dessert to the table – apple crumble made by yours truly at the weekend – I casually mentioned that I had another piece of news.

'Is it about your Maths mocks?' she asked.

So tedious! I'm taking a couple of GCSE subjects early and it's all she wants to talk about! Instead I filled her in about the trip. 'All the girls are coming – Lucy's the only one out of us who's skied before so the rest of us can be beginners together,' I told her. 'It's a really good opportunity for me to learn a new skill.' Those kinds of words, opportunity and new skill, usually work like magic with Mum . . . but not this time. She put down her spoon and looked at me in surprise.

'I'm sorry, Hermione, but this isn't an option for you right now. How could you think it would be? Paw Paw is coming to visit that week, remember, and she'll want to see you. Besides, you've just spent the Christmas holidays messing around with those girls. Now it's time for you to settle down and focus on your work.'

Next she realized that the ski trip was my birthday week and tried to imply that I would have a better time with her and Paw Paw! (I haven't told the girls about my birthday because fuss = embarrassing.)

Then she started talking about stuff we could do with Paw Paw and THAT was basically the end of the discussion. I kept my cool downstairs, but now I'm upstairs, fuming. Hey – hang on, why is it only Mum's decision?

I have two parents, don't I?

This divorce is the worst!

Hermione x

23:34

Hermione: Hey, Dad. Are you there? xx

'What do you MEAN, you're not allowed to come?' asked Abby in horror the next morning. The girls had gathered together at break-time to add their names to the sign-up sheet. Hermione gulped. How was she going to explain this? She felt as if she might burst into tears.

'Is it a money thing?' asked Jessie sympathetically. The school had arranged a package deal to keep the costs as low as possible, but for some families the trip was out of the question – with ski-equipment hire and lift passes plus travel, food and accommodation, it wasn't cheap.

Hermione shook her head. 'It's not really about that,' she mumbled, tucking a lock of too-short hair behind her ear. It immediately fell out again. *Stupid hair*. 'My mum just wants me to focus on work, and my grandmother is coming to visit at half-term.'

'Doesn't Paw Paw usually s-stay for a couple of m-months, though?' asked Lucy. 'I'm sure they c-can cope without you f-for one week!' She linked arms with Hermione. 'I can't believe this! What d-did your dad say?'

'He, er, he doesn't know about it yet,' said Hermione quietly.

'Oh, right,' said Abby, nodding. 'It's probably not the easiest time for your parents to send you away.' Then she flushed, her eyes widening as Hermione stared at her in dismay. 'Well, it won't be the same without you, H,' Abby continued quickly, trying to gloss over her slip-up.

'Hang on!' said Jessie. 'What did you mean, it's not the best time?' She looked questioningly at Lucy, who shrugged.

'As in, like, Hermione's parents, well . . .' Abby floundered.

Hermione sighed. 'Sorry, Abs. I've put you in an awkward position . . . Luce, Jessie – you might as well know.' She took a deep breath, tugging at a loose string on her school jumper. 'My parents are getting divorced. It really sucks. My dad has moved out and my mum's morphed into a complete monster.' Hermione avoided Lucy's eye. They were best friends and she felt guilty about not telling Lucy first.

'WHAAAT?' cried Jessie. 'When did this happen?'

'Over the last couple of weeks.' Hermione paused as she sniffed an ominous vanilla scent and then spotted Dakota approaching the noticeboard. She lowered her voice. If their arch nemesis got hold of the information she would be sure to taunt her with it. 'Abs came round on the day I found out, just before Christmas, so I told her.' She finally met Lucy's eye who looked surprised, and definitely a bit hurt. 'I've been planning to tell you guys ever since, but honestly I just want to forget that it's even happening! It's much more fun to focus on vlogging!' She tried to put on a brave smile.

There was a brief pause as they watched Dakota sign her name on the sheet. 'Ben's coming too,' she said

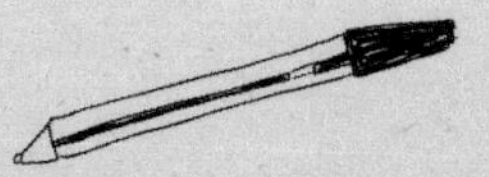

loudly to her friend Kayleigh. 'This will be our first trip together – I can't wait!'

'Cute,' nodded Kayleigh. 'Now it's my turn to find a bae.'

Hermione noticed Abby turn pale. So Ben and Dakota *were* officially together?

'Such a shame Ameeka can't afford it – how embarrassing,' Dakota continued, passing Kayleigh the pen. She smugly tossed her shiny brown hair.

Hermione and her friends exchanged shocked glances. 'We don't all have unlimited access to Daddy's funds, Dakota,' called Jessie. 'Nice way to talk about your friend too!'

'Do me a favour and butt out of my business,' retorted Dakota, turning to face them. 'How unfortunate that most of you seem to be coming on the trip, but, then again, it might be good for a laugh! Wow – why are you all looking so miserable?'

Hermione froze. Would anyone let slip about the divorce?

'Nothing you'd understand,' snapped Abby.

'Nothing you'd WANT to understand, I bet,' smirked Kayleigh. 'Loser problems anonymous – they probably just caught sight of themselves in the mirror.'

They sauntered off in a sea of giggles, and Hermione felt relief sweep over her.

'I'm really sorry about your parents, H,' Jessie said. 'But it's SO WRONG that you're not coming on the ski trip. Girls Can Vlog on tour is just what you need right now.'

'It is,' agreed Lucy. She smiled at Hermione. 'Plus I think y-you'd love skiing, and the mountains. You know what M-Morgan would say – don't take no for an answer! Is it worth one m-more try?'

10:04

Dad: Sorry, I didn't pick up your message until now. What's up, sweetie? Dad x

VLOG 2

FADE IN: NIGHT-TIME IN HERMIONE'S BEDROOM.

HERMIONE is standing by a bookcase, wearing cupcake-print pyjama bottoms and a grey T-shirt with a logo on saying: *So many books, so little time.*

HERMIONE

Hi, everyone! As you probably all know, I LOVE reading so I'm going to talk about my favourite books and characters today.

I'm subscribed to dozens of BookTubers who do amazing book hauls and reviews. I'm pretty new to it myself, but one day I hope publishers will send me books to review. That would be so cool! Is this still filming?

(she checks the camera anxiously)

Phew! I'm still getting used to my new camera.

(she strokes her hand along the top shelf of books)

So, firstly, here are my most precious books, which I would grab if my house was burning down! There are some first editions and books that have been signed by authors: Suzanne Collins, Philip Pullman, J. K. Rowling, Zoella and a few more.

(she sits down on her bed with a pile of books by her side)

Next up, I want to talk about my favourite kick-ass characters, who all happen to be girls. Woo! Sometimes book characters seem more real to me than actual people – does anyone else get that?

(she looks awkwardly into the camera)

No? Maybe it's just me? Anyway, here goes!

(she holds up a book)

Number one: Lucy from *The Lion, the Witch and the Wardrobe* by C. S. Lewis.

Who else wishes that they could go to Narnia and have magical adventures with Aslan the lion?

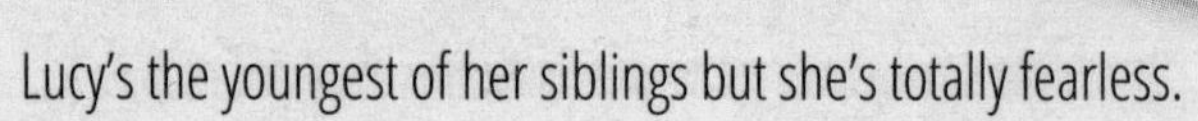

Lucy's the youngest of her siblings but she's totally fearless. When I first read this, I tried walking into a wardrobe in my grandmother's house to find the surprise doorway into Narnia. Cringe!

(she holds up another book)

Next, it's *Pippi Longstocking* by Astrid Lindgren. Pippi is just so crazy, rebellious and she lives in a house all on her own with a pet monkey. Plus she has amazing braids – I'm jealous.

(sadly pats her short bob, holds up another book)

Moving on, *Matilda* by Roald Dahl. Like me, Matilda loves reading and also – she has superpowers! When I first read this aged seven, I tried to make a spoon lift into the air like she does, with just the power of thought. Hashtag *fail*!

CUT TO: A pre-recorded clip of a spoon being pulled into the air with a visible string.

HERMIONE (CONTINUED)

Ha ha! Close enough!

Next up, Dorothy from

The Wonderful Wizard of Oz.

(holds up another book)

Did you know it was a book before it was a movie? Another brave girl who's transported to a magic land and has amazing adventures.

(she giggles)

Do you see a recurring theme here? Magic for the win!

(she holds up another book)

Someone less magic-y but so relatable is Margaret from Judy Blume's *Are You There God? It's Me, Margaret.* Even though this was written in, like, 1970, I really identify with Margaret and all her embarrassing secrets and dreams. She's obsessed with bras!

CUT TO: Shot of several of bras being thrown into the air.

HERMIONE (CONTINUED)

Those are not mine by the way – they're my mum's!

(glances at the pile of paperbacks which is down to two books)

Nearly there! Next is Katniss Everdeen of *The Hunger Games.*

(she holds up another book)

She's the ultimate badass: brave, a talented archer and never intimidated by boys. Not that I'd want to spend my life firing arrows from trees, but, you know.

And, like Pippi, amazing braid goals.

(she pauses)

Finally, last but not least – and no prizes for guessing – is Hermione Granger, the brightest witch of her age!

(she stands and beams, holding the book up)

From Harry Potter, for those of you who have been living under a rock your entire lives. I'm not actually named after her, but

I do think we're quite similar. We're both a bit shy when you first meet us, we love reading and MOST IMPORTANTLY we always save the day. And, of course, we both love Harry!

(she grins)

So, those are my top kick-ass characters; it was really hard to narrow them down. Let me know your favourites in the comments down below.

(she waves)

See you soon, my little house-elves! Oh, we promised a shout-out to the best New Year's goal, which goes to . . . Lovecats13 for pledging one hundred hours of volunteering at her local cat rescue centre. Amazing!

FADE OUT.

Views: 759

Subscribers: 5,100

Comments:

BookGeek: My kick-ass character is Anne of Green Gables. Green hair! LOL

lucylocket: That Matilda thing is sooooo cute!

Sammylovesbooks: I love Poison Ivy from DC Comics . . . 

ShyGirl1: My fave is Jo from *Little Women*.

pink_sparkles: Katniss rules!

my_cute_bookshelf: Which Hermione were you named after?

HashtagHermione: The Hermione in *A Winter's Tale* by Shakespeare – nobody's ever heard of her, lol

(scroll down to see 27 more comments)

Chapter Three

07:43

Hermione: I CAN COME I CAN COME ☺

Lucy: What happened??

Hermione: Long story short: Dad convinced Mum. 

Lucy: YESSSSSS

Hermione: It took ages, but in the end he persuaded her I deserved a treat cos of everything with the divorce – guilt factor!

Lucy: Have you signed up? Thought deadline was last week?

Hermione: Dad called school and they added me just in time.

Lucy: So cool ☺

Hermione: Also, Dad's given me some ££ to get some ski gear.

Lucy: I'll give you the list of everything you need – you're gonna look amazing!

Hermione: Ha ha not sure! At least ski helmet will cover stupid hair! Gotta go message the others now xx

Lucy: Thanks for telling me first. ❤
WOOHOO! GIRLS CAN VLOG ON TOUR!

'And what about Chemistry, are you confident with the periodic table?'

'Yes, Mum,' groaned Hermione, watching her mother arrange flowers on the kitchen table. 'That poster you put on my bedroom wall really helped drum it in. Can I please go now?' Mrs Chan removed a couple of leaves from the vase, frowned, then started putting them back in again.

'Hmm, does that look better?' she fretted. 'No, I'm going to have to start again.'

'Mum, relax – they look great,' said Hermione impatiently, getting to her feet.

Her mother glanced at her. 'I have my standards, Hermione. Just because your father isn't around doesn't mean we can't live in a pleasant and well-ordered space.' She removed the dripping bunch of flowers and laid them out on the table. 'Speaking of which, how is your book tidying going? Have you boxed up those extra books for the charity shop?'

Hermione sighed, edging towards the door. She'd tidied one section of her room for her vlog but not the bit that was out of shot. 'I'm working on it,

Mum – you know I am. Besides, it's my room. Nobody else has to live with the mess. And it's only books – you should see Abby's room!'

'Hmm, littered with make-up and silly clothes, no doubt, knowing that girl,' sniffed her mother as Hermione's phone pinged. 'She could use a periodic table poster too, I imagine.'

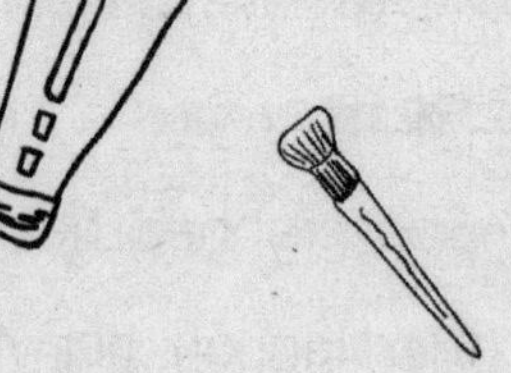

11:27

Lucy: Where r u???

11:28

Hermione: Trying to escape!! Mum is in MEGA MONSTER MODE today!

Hermione sent the message then stuffed her phone in her rucksack. 'Seriously, Mum, please can I go? Lucy's waiting for me at the bus stop.'

Mrs Chan gave the flowers a long look then started placing them back in the vase. 'Fine,' she said. 'Don't

forget I need you back here by four. And don't buy things you don't need – stick to the essentials for the trip. You girls are so frivolous, with your make-up, your shoes, your—'

'I promise, OK?' Hermione said impatiently, interrupting her. 'Wow, no wonder Dad moved out,' she muttered, turning away to root through the coat rack. 'You suck the fun out of everything . . . You probably drove him away.'

She grabbed her jacket, then froze, catching the expression on her mother's face. *Oh no.* Hermione hadn't meant to say that last bit so loudly. But it was obvious that her mother had heard every word.

'Well, Hermione,' said Mrs Chan after a chilly pause. 'I'm sorry you feel that way. However, it may one day occur to you that I am not solely responsible for our . . . parting ways. Your father's not perfect, either.' She looked like she wanted to say more about this, but the next words were a change of subject. 'Essentials only, remember.'

'I promise,' said Hermione sullenly, looking down at her trainers as her mother walked out of the room. She felt guilty, and incredibly confused. Minutes later it was a massive relief to be out in the fresh cold air, heading towards her friends, gossip and shopping.

'I can't believe it's only a few weeks away,' said Jessie as the girls queued up for hot chocolates in the cafe at the mall. They'd decided it was important to top up their energy levels before shopping. 'Extra whipped cream, please,' she told the server.

'It can't come fast enough,' said Hermione, reaching for a white-chocolate-fudge cookie. 'Even though I'm kind of nervous about the actual skiing.'

'Don't worry, we'll be naturals,' said Abby confidently. 'How hard can it be? It's all downhill!'

Hermione smiled. She didn't think it was quite that simple. 'Let's hope you're right. Anyway, I'd go on an extreme skydiving trip at the moment to escape my parents.' They paid and found a table. 'Jess, you're so brave to try snowboarding!'

Jessie took a gulp of her hot chocolate. 'Wow, that's hot!' She put it back down carefully then grinned at Hermione. 'Yeah, well, I love skateboarding and I hear it's pretty similar. Plus it means I'm allowed to use all the lingo – WIPEOUT! That means stacking it in a major way.'

Hermione gulped. She didn't want to think about that.

'And you guys are "plankers" – which means skiers,' Jessie continued. 'My board is a "lunch tray".'

'Right on!' giggled Lucy.

'OK, cool kids, can we PLEASE talk about shopping now,' said Abby.

'Yeah, there's a lot we need to get,' said Lucy. 'M-most of my ski stuff doesn't fit any more and you guys are all newbies.'

'Don't remind me,' groaned Hermione.

'I've got some of Leon's kit,' said Jessie, pulling a face. 'He went a couple of years ago. Unfortunately I don't think any of it's been washed since then.'

Abby reached into her handbag. 'I brought the school list of what we need to pack – ew!' She pulled out a crumpled piece of paper, which was covered with sticky lipgloss. 'I knew that tube of Beige Babe wasn't closing properly! It's gone everywhere!'

Hermione giggled and passed her a napkin. 'I've got the list here too,' she said, taking out a notebook. 'I also jotted down some tips I got from RedVelvet's tutorial about packing for a ski trip.' One thing Hermione loved about YouTube was the way there was always the perfect video to helped you organize your life, no matter what you were doing. She frowned in concentration. 'We need our ski gear, but also snacks and toiletries. Mini shampoos, shower gel, sun cream, lip balm with SPF . . .'

'Also BB cream with SPF,' chipped in Abby, cleaning the lipgloss off her wallet. 'Ooh, and waterproof mascara.'

'OK, but maybe we should s-start with actual skiwear.' Lucy grinned. 'Also, if anyone needs an après-ski outfit, this is the time t-to think about it.'

'What's "apray ski"?' asked Abby. 'Is that a different sort of skiing? Like a super-advanced level?'

Lucy laughed. 'In a way . . . It m-means "after skiing" in French. It's the t-time at the end of the day when you've come off the slopes and get to hang out, s-socialize, have dinner . . . it's really fun cos everyone goes.'

Abby's eyes lit up. 'And you have a complete outfit change for this?'

'I'm just planning to take some leggings and a hoodie,' said Jessie, draining her drink. 'We'll probably be totally exhausted after hours on the slopes.' But Hermione could tell that Abby had zoned out and was already planning some amazing outfits. After all, Ben was coming on this trip – even though he was officially with Dakota now and they were PDAing all over the place . . .

They finished their drinks. 'This place will have most of the stuff we need,' said Jessie, leading them down the escalator towards a large sportswear shop. 'I come here to get my gymnastics kit sometimes – you can pick up some real bargains!'

As they wound their way through the skiwear department, something caught Hermione's eye.

'Is that – is that Miss Piercy?' she asked Lucy.

'Where? Oh right, sitting over there outside the f-fitting rooms? Yeah! She looks like she's waiting for s-someone.'

Hermione squirmed. 'This is kind of embarrassing. Shall we come back later?'

'MISS!' yelled Jessie, noticing her too. 'MISS! Over here!'

'Or not . . .' trailed off Hermione. Even though she really liked Miss Piercy, she always found it weird seeing teachers outside of school, when you were expected to chat to them about non-school stuff. Like they were just regular people.

Miss Piercy glanced over, her eyebrows rising in surprise at the sight of her students.

She looks embarrassed too, thought Hermione.

'Girls, hello! What are you – well, I suppose I can guess. Picking up some skiwear for the trip?'

'You know it, miss. There is SO much to get,' said Abby dramatically.

'Well, there's a big selection and—'

'How about these, Annabel?' interrupted a male voice.

The girls gasped as they looked up. It was Mr Byrne, their new Physics teacher, who'd stepped out of the changing room without noticing them. He'd started at the school after Christmas, replacing Ms Henry, who had decided to leave after an incident involving the disappearance of laboratory supplies.

Hermione thought Mr Byrne was a nice teacher, but she knew that the others found him a bit of a joke – he was kind of nervous and clumsy. And now the sight of him did make her want to laugh. He was standing before them in neon green salopettes (waterproof skiing trousers held up by braces, Lucy had explained). These were bunched up over his jeans and shirt, obviously several sizes too small. His jeans had ridden up on one side displaying a section of pale, hairy leg

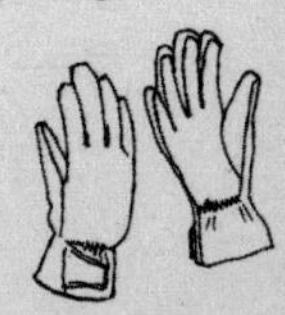

and the colour of the salopettes did very little for his ghostly complexion. Tiny beads of sweat had formed on his brow, and as he caught sight of the girls a small whimper escaped his mouth. 'Hello, ladies – how, er, nice to see you!'

'Hi, Mr Byrne!' chorused Abby and Jessie before spluttering something about going to check out the thermals and rushing off in not particularly subtle fits of laughter. Abby pulled out her phone and texted feverishly as she went. Hermione knew she was messaging all their classmates.

Mr Byrne glanced anxiously at Miss Piercy, then at Hermione and Lucy. 'You see – I'm still rather new to town so Miss Piercy kindly offered to help me kit myself out. For the ski trip.'

'He didn't know where any shops were,' explained Miss Piercy, turning a bit pink.

'Well, that was very nice of you to help him, miss,' said Hermione politely, after a slight pause. She nudged Lucy, who was standing silently beside her, staring at the neon apparition in front of them. 'And that colour is, er, very striking on you, sir. Anyway, we'd better catch up with the others. See you in school.'

'You are s-such a teacher's pet,' said Lucy fondly as they walked away. 'I c-couldn't speak because I was worried I would l-laugh.' She glanced back at the teachers. 'I mean, how are we going to c-cope with seeing him in that outfit every day for a week?'

VLOG 3

FADE IN: ABBY'S ROOM – EVENING.

ABBY in her room with a huge pile of clothes, shoes and toiletries on the bed. Behind her is an open chest of drawers and a wardrobe with clothes spilling out on to the floor. An empty suitcase sits on the floor.

ABBY

Hey, Hermione! I didn't hear you! I just switched the camera on.

HERMIONE

(entering the room with her own suitcase)

Probably because of your singing. I did knock! Josh let me in.

Hi, guys!

(she waves to the camera)

ABBY

So Hermione's arrived just in time to help me sort through this mess. I don't even know where to start!

HERMIONE

(shaking her head in an exaggerated way)

Hmmm. Looks like a tornado just swept through here . . . Where's the stuff you're taking?

ABBY

(waving her arms about)

Well, it's sort of everywhere . . . I mean, I haven't decided what to take yet, but I don't think I'll have enough room.

HERMIONE

Not unless you're bringing a second suitcase . . . we're only going for a week, you know!

ABBY

(batting her eyelashes)

Oh, H, can you please just do it for me? Pretty please? You're so organized and good at this sort of thing . . .

HERMIONE

Abs, flattery will get you nowhere! You've got to do it yourself – but I will help.

HERMIONE puts her case on the bed and opens it up. Everything is neatly folded and stored in the correct compartments.

HERMIONE (CONTINUED)

See? This is what you want to aim for . . .

ABBY

(shrieking)

That is amazing! I'd never be able to do that!

HERMIONE

I learned it from that RedVelvet video. I think it was called Ski Trip: Packing Like a Pro. We'll link it down below. You see how I've got compartments for my toiletries in small bottles, and separate Ziplocs for my underwear and socks so they don't get lost. Anyway, let's have a go at yours.

(she pulls out a list)

Two pairs of thermal leggings, two pairs of long-sleeved thermal tops, two zip-up fleeces, your brand-new salopettes – oh, they're really cute! You can travel in your ski jacket.

ABBY is leaping around the room finding the items mentioned and HERMIONE is folding them neatly into a pile.

HERMIONE (CONTINUED)

Now ski gloves, goggles, socks, beanies and your buff or scarf.

ABBY

Have you seen all these cute hats I've got?

(modelling one)

I went a bit crazy . . .

HERMIONE

Very nice, but, Abs, you've got too many. Choose two, max! Now, let's sort out your PJs, underwear and then try to figure out your après-ski outfits.

ABBY

Après-ski. That's the most important part . . . gotta look sophisticated for those French boys! Isn't this cute?

(holds up a black sequinned top)

The door bursts open and JOSH enters.

JOSH

What's this about French boys? I thought you were supposed to be learning to ski, not snogging French boys . . . Charlie might get jealous!

ABBY lunges at JOSH and swats him with her ski gloves.

ABBY

SHUT UP! What are you doing here anyway?

JOSH

(snatches the top and holds it up)

Seriously – you must be trying to impress someone with this little number!

ABBY

JOSH, GO AWAY!

(bats him again)

HERMIONE

Actually, that's in the 'stay at home' pile, Josh. Don't worry. It's all under control.

JOSH

Well, Abs, at least you've got one sensible friend. TRY not to get into trouble so you get sent home or arrested!

ABBY

(sarcastically)

Ha ha, as if . . . anyway, why are you here?

JOSH

(bows mockingly)

Mademoiselles, dinner is served!

CUT TO: a sped-up clip of a clock face with the hands spinning round from 7 p.m. to 8 p.m.

TRANSITION TO: ABBY sitting on her suitcase trying to get it to close and HERMIONE helping.

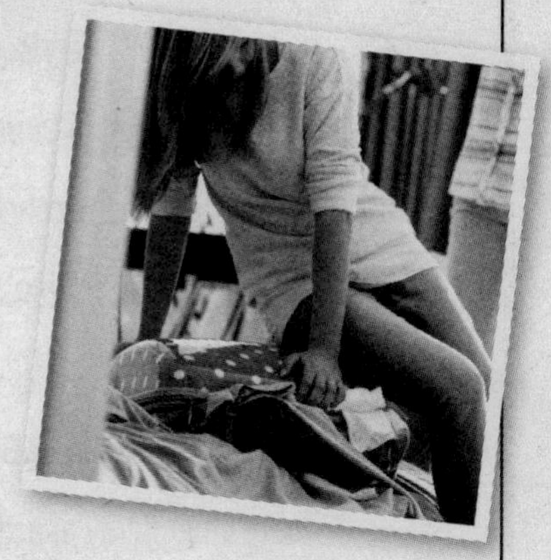

ABBY

Sorry, everyone, we had to go and have dinner!

HERMIONE

Abs, I really think you should take out those stilettos . . .

ABBY

Not happening . . . anyway . . .

(turns to camera)

I hope you all enjoyed sharing our packing experience and a special *merci* (see, I can even speak some French) to the AMAZING Hermione who rescued me from disaster!

HERMIONE

(laughs)

We're going to be vlogging our whole ski trip, starting with the 5 a.m. (eek!) start on the coach tomorrow. So don't forget to check your subscription boxes for regular videos!

ABBY

There'll be plenty of action, I promise! *Au revoir!*

(they both wave to camera)

FADE OUT.

Views: 1,354

Subscribers: 5,207

Comments:

***jazzyjessie*:** Can't wait till tomorrow, guys.

lucylocket: LOL. Repacking my bag too!

awesomeannie: SO JEL! My school has a school trip, but my parents say we can't afford it. ☹

queen_dakota: Pigsty! Rubbish room, rubbish vlog.

StalkerGurl: More Josh, please!

MagicMorgan: Wish I was coming too xx

SassySays: Ha ha – I have big struggles with packing too!

(scroll down to see 62 more comments)

Chapter Four

'See ya,' drawled Dakota to her parents as she stepped on to the coach in her expensive ski jacket with fur-trimmed hood. 'I'll text you if I need any extra cash.'

'Goodbye, princess!' they called in unison, waving proudly. Dakota's mum rushed up and gave her a kiss on the cheek, pausing to wipe off the fluorescent pink lipstick with a tissue before Dakota pushed her away.

'Please!' she said in disgust. 'It's only for six days.'

Hermione grinned. She was glad she'd been dropped off by Abby's mum, not that her parents would be that embarrassing in a million years. They weren't into public displays of affection. In fact, she thought, her heart sinking, they would probably never wave her off anywhere ever again, now that they couldn't stand to be in the same room together. She pictured herself heading off to university in a few years' time, alone at the train station, surrounded by bags and unable to carry them—

'Have you remembered your camera?' asked Abby, interrupting her gloomy thoughts.

Hermione held up her rucksack. 'Right here, alongside my delicious vanilla cream cupcakes.' She'd stayed up late earlier in the week baking some of her favourite recipes. Ever since the news of the divorce, she'd found baking to be a soothing distraction, almost as good as writing in her diary.

A groggy-looking Miss Piercy approached them with a clipboard. 'Right, Abby, Hermione, have you loaded your luggage? Yes?' They nodded. 'Fine, please board the coach and I'll tick you both off. Yes, Kayleigh, what is it?'

'Are we stopping at KFC, miss?' asked Kayleigh,

dragging her bag along the ground.

The teacher glanced up from her clipboard with a confused expression. 'What?'

'KFC,' said Kayleigh, panting as she half threw the bag at the bus driver who was helping to load the luggage on to the coach. 'You know, at the service station. Soon we'll only be getting rank French food so it might be our last chance to have something normal.'

'French food is delicious,' muttered Hermione, dreaming of mountains of croissants and huge plates of cheese. She'd never been to France before and she couldn't wait to try the local delicacies.

'French food is delicious,' mimicked Kayleigh, giving Hermione a dirty look. 'So, miss? KFC? Zinger Burger? Yes or no?'

Miss Piercy closed her eyes. 'Kayleigh, it's five o'clock in the morning. How you can think of fried chicken is beyond me.' She sighed. 'What I need right now is a large dose of caffeine. But, yes, we'll be making regular stops and I promise you won't starve.'

Kayleigh looked put out and without really knowing why, Hermione said, 'I've got some cupcakes if you want one?' She opened her rucksack to show her.

'Not exactly a full meal, is it?' said Kayleigh, taking a brief look. 'They're not even that big.' She stomped on to the coach. 'Your hair still looks weird, by the way,' she called as she went.

Abby sighed. 'That was asking for trouble, H. Of course she would never take one of your cupcakes. Sometimes you're too nice for your own good!'

Mr Byrne hurried over, wearing a tangerine orange ski jacket and holding out a Styrofoam cup. 'I couldn't help overhearing,' he began, looking at Miss Piercy. 'About the caffeine, that is. Please have my cappuccino, Annabel.' The eager expression on his face reminded Hermione of a puppy desperate for attention. 'Do take it – I already had one at home. It's no trouble – whoops!' In his eagerness he sloshed some coffee over Abby. Hermione cringed in sympathy at his awkwardness.

'Don't worry, sir,' Abby giggled. 'Just my brand-new ski

jacket, specially purchased for this trip. Oh well, at least it's machine washable! Come on, H – let's find some seats at the back.' She lowered her voice. 'Is he going to wear that jacket with the green salopettes we saw him in? I don't know if my eyes will be able to take it! Lucky I bought those new sunglasses!'

As they boarded the coach, Hermione turned and saw Miss Piercy gratefully accept the coffee with a big smile, which Mr Byrne returned. It was actually kind of cute. She wondered if Miss Piercy was single. *OMG, why am I thinking about my teacher's love life?* she asked herself. *My parents' divorce must be sending me loopy. Good thing I'm having some time away!* She waved out of the window at Lucy and Jessie who had arrived with Lucy's dad.

Hermione followed Abby to the very back, a few rows behind Dakota and Ben, who were eating sweets and taking selfies.

'Those two are getting ridiculous,' she whispered, as Dakota stuck her phone out into the aisle for the best

angle. Ben planted a kiss on her cheek while running his hand through his hair.

'Which two?' said Abby, sitting down and checking her phone.

Hermione smiled fondly. 'You know exactly which two. Dakota and Ben. I mean, "Bakota".' Kayleigh had come up with the name and Dakota was now using it as a hashtag on all her Instagram posts. It was the worst thing Hermione had ever seen. '*Bakota* – it sounds like bacteria! Do they honestly think they're like a celebrity couple?'

'Who cares,' said Abby, shrugging. 'Why are we talking about them when we have like a million vlogs to plan?' Her eyes widened. 'Ooh, the one from last night already has so many views! Awesome! This trip could take us to over six thousand subscribers.' She high-fived Hermione.

'Your bedroom looked like a pigsty in that stupid video,' shouted Kayleigh, sitting across the aisle from Dakota and Ben. A few other kids, who had obviously

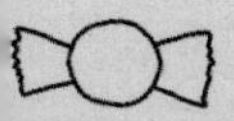

also seen the video, broke into laughter. 'You need to sort your life out!' Kayleigh continued.

Hermione sighed. 'Always so negative, Kayleigh. So what if Abby's not the neatest?' She usually felt uncomfortable speaking up in group situations, but today she was too happy to care. 'Anyway, thanks for the views! Good to know you're still subscribed.'

Abby squealed with delight and Ben chuckled. 'She's got you there! Hey, Abs, they say living like a pig is a sign of creativity, anyway.' He was soon silenced by a look from Dakota.

Does Ben still like Abby? wondered Hermione. He still teased her all the time – wasn't that a type of flirting? Or did he just enjoy winding her up? She sighed. Boys! So annoying . . . She reached into her bag for the copy of *Harry Potter and the Philosopher's Stone* that she liked to carry as a good-luck charm when travelling. *Apart from you, Harry!* she thought, smiling at the battered cover.

*

'Miss Piercy says there's still forty minutes to go until we reach the Eurotunnel,' reported Jessie a few hours later, returning to her seat. She took out her games console. 'Which means . . . time for at least one more game of Fifa! KSI would be proud.'

'You're obsessed,' said Hermione fondly. She and Lucy were reading magazines and Abby was touching up her make-up while singing along loudly to Taylor Swift, just one earphone in so that she could still chat to them.

This is brilliant, thought Hermione. After the last few weeks, and that upsetting conversation with her mum, it felt amazing to be on holiday, surrounded by her friends, eating sweets and messing around. It was already the best trip ever. Plus, no actual – terrifying – skiing yet! The coach buzzed with shouts and laughter.

'Hey, Dakota, hungry yet? You want an onion ring?' called Kayleigh, dangling one in her friend's face. They'd stopped at a service station for a late breakfast, but Dakota hadn't wanted anything.

Dakota waved it away. 'That stinks,' she snapped. 'And your breath is gross, Kayleigh.' She yawned and cleared her throat. 'Leave me alone. I'm trying to sleep.'

'Erm, guys,' said Abby, speaking loudly because of the music in her ear. 'Is it me, or is Dakota looking REALLY unwell?' Hermione glanced at Dakota who was indeed as pale as skimmed milk, her long-lashed eyes closed. She gave a small burp and covered her mouth with her hand.

Ben unfastened his seat belt and stood up. 'Kayleigh, I think Dakota . . . might . . . uh . . . need you. Here, take my place.' He came and sat in a spare seat near Abby. Hermione eyed him suspiciously.

'Mind if I plug in?' he asked. Hermione nudged Lucy, as Abby shrugged and handed him the spare earphone.

'SCORE!' Jessie looked up from tapping furiously at her game and noticed Ben. 'Why is he sitting with us?' she mouthed to Hermione, her eyes widening.

'He-he just wants to get away in case

Dakota spews on him,' whispered Lucy, as the same time as Miss Piercy said loudly, 'Oh dear – Dakota, are you all right?'

The whole coach went quiet as the teacher walked down the aisle and everyone realized that something was wrong. Kayleigh moved next to Dakota and was fanning her face with a greasy napkin.

Someone squealed, 'Oh no, I hate it when people get travel sick.'

'I'm fine –' snapped Dakota, opening her eyes. 'Kayleigh, get that disgusting rag away from me.' She burped again, louder than last time, then casually ran her fingers through her hair as if nothing was wrong.

Hermione caught Abby's eye and stifled a giggle, while Ben shuddered.

'Maybe take this plastic bag just in case,' said Miss Piercy, holding one out to the pale girl. 'Driver, we may need to stop in a minute.'

'I said I'm fine,' mumbled Dakota weakly. She turned as if to say something to Kayleigh and then suddenly was sick everywhere. It went all over Kayleigh's lap and into her open rucksack.

The coach erupted into shrieks of laughter and dismay as the awful smell permeated the stuffy air of the coach. Kayleigh was speechless with shock, staring at Dakota in horror.

'OK, folks, no need to panic,' said Mr Byrne, standing up, and, Hermione noticed, looking rather green himself. 'We're going to pull over in a minute and get this sorted out, then we can be on our way again. Miss Piercy, here are some wipes.' He walked over to Miss Piercy, handed them over then, as Dakota threw up again, hurried back to his seat.

'I can't breathe,' muttered Ben. 'That STINKS.'

Abby gave a little shrug. 'It's probably that awful vanilla perfume she wears. That would turn anyone's stomach after a while.' She glanced at Ben mischievously. 'No Bakota selfie to capture the moment, then?'

Hermione giggled. You couldn't blame Abby for being smug after the hard time Dakota had given her during the *Grease* rehearsals. Not to mention the Ben situation. She watched as Miss Piercy did her best to mop up Dakota and Kayleigh, who was still frozen like a vomit-covered statue.

This is the most brilliant trip ever! thought Hermione again, resisting the urge to film the sorry pair.

VLOG 4

LUCY

(voiceover)

Hi, guys! So this is the edited h-highlights of day one of the amazing s-ski trip. We t-took turns filming on the unbelievably long coach trip and here are some of the f-funniest moments.

CUT TO: View out of the bus window of motorway and scenery and then panning the interior of the bus. About forty kids sprawled on seats, laughing and chatting or listening to headphones. DAKOTA is napping, wrapped in a blanket with a pink satin sleep mask on.

The camera closes in on HERMIONE reading, ABBY wearing headphones and putting on some make-up and JESSIE playing on her games console.

JESSIE

Yay, maxed that!

(puts down console)

OK – I have a game for us to play. Who's in?

HERMIONE

(her nose in a book)

Sorry, just got to a good bit . . .

ABBY

I'm in! What is it?

JESSIE

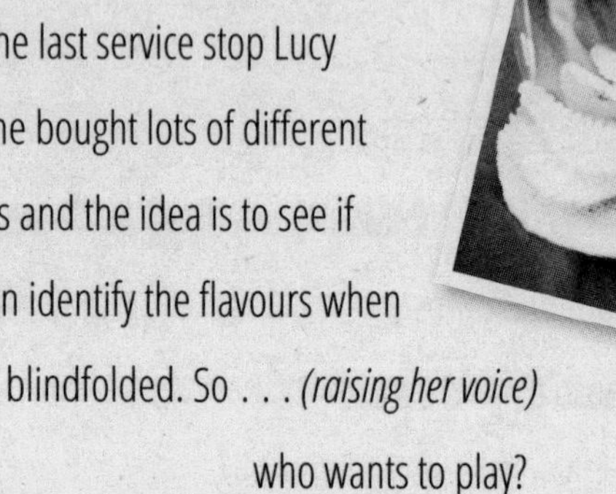

It's called the Crisp Challenge. At the last service stop Lucy and me bought lots of different crisps and the idea is to see if you can identify the flavours when blindfolded. So . . . *(raising her voice)* who wants to play?

BEN

I do! Sounds easy! You in, Eric?

ERIC

(looking uncertainly at the camera)

Is this going on your vlog? Er, go on, then . . .

ABBY

OK, you two play each other for the first round. We need some blindfolds . . . Here's my scarf and, Ben, why don't you borrow Dakota's sleep mask? That would work!

BEN leans over and takes off DAKOTA's sleep mask. DAKOTA scowls but lets him take it. BEN puts it on.

ABBY

Cute!

JESSIE

OK, here we go . . . Open up . . .

(feeds the blindfolded Ben and Eric a crisp each)

BEN

(chewing)

Oh, I know. Bacon, smoky bacon.

ERIC

Hmm. Maybe . . . but it's cheesy too.

I'd say cheese and bacon.

JESSIE

Nice one, Eric! You're right.

ABBY

Is that actually a flavour? Yuck! Next . . .

(feeds them each another crisp)

ERIC

(chewing)

Spicy . . . barbecue? Or maybe even jalapeño?

BEN

Hot, hot! I need some water . . . Yeah, jalapeño!

JESSIE

(cheering)

Both right. Here's another . . .

BEN

Yuck!

(spits crisp out in his hand)

Prawn cocktail. I HATE prawn cocktail.

ABBY

(giggling)

All right, Ben! Calm down!

ERIC

(grabbing the whole bag)

I love prawn cocktail.

JESSIE

OK, last but not least . . .

ERIC

Hmm. Is that . . . Marmite?

BEN

No! Wait – I know . . .

Worcestershire sauce.

JESSIE

Are you sure? Final answers, please!

BEN

(spraying crumbs everywhere)

Worcestershire sauce!

ERIC

Marmite!

JESSIE

Game over, Ben! And the winner is Eric! Perfect score!

ABBY

Never mind, Ben! Have a crisp!

(she tries to force-feed him a prawn cocktail crisp from ERIC's bag)

DAKOTA

(sounding annoyed)

Ben, come over here right now! I need my mask back. You're sooo childish!

BEN scuttles back to sit with DAKOTA.

DAKOTA (CONTINUED)

Ew – your breath is terrible!

CUT TO: LATER

Camera pans inside the bus. MISS PIERCY sleeping with her head leaning on MR BYRNE's shoulder. DAKOTA sitting on her own and asleep. BEN snoring in a seat across the aisle, using his ski jacket as a blanket.

LUCY

(whispering)

So it's now a lot later. There was a b-bit of an . . . 'incident' and we had to make an unplanned s-stop. It's lucky that there's no smell-o-vision with this film as the aroma on the b-bus is pretty rank! And everyone is getting a bit bored . . .

Camera focuses on ABBY who slips into the seat next to BEN. She is holding an eyeliner pencil. After a few seconds she touches BEN's cheek lightly with the eyeliner and makes a tiny dot. BEN doesn't move so she does it again. This happens a few times with ABBY smiling and trying not to laugh.

BEN wakes up suddenly.

BEN

(sleepily)

Hi! What are you doing here?

ABBY

I had to move seats . . . Hermione wanted to lie down. Do you mind?

BEN

No, no . . . I just thought there was a fly.

(pulls up ski jacket, turns away and closes eyes)

ABBY waits a little while and then starts drawing on BEN's cheek again.

CUT TO: shot of BEN with 'I ❤ Justin Bieber' drawn on his cheek.

ERIC

(walking down the aisle – he stops by BEN,

then laughs out loud)

Hey, bro! Wake up!

You'd better have a look at yourself!

ABBY hands BEN a make-up mirror while giggling.

BEN

What the –?

(starts rubbing his cheek and smearing the make-up)

Don't tell me you're filming this?

JESSIE

Maybe . . . Wait and see!

BEN leaps up and places a hand over the camera lens.

FADE OUT.

Views: 2,657

Subscribers: 6,103

Comments:

funnyinternetperson54: hahahaha

Shygirl1: Marmite crisps give me life!

PrankingsteinJosh: LMSO

awesomeannie: Really jel now! Looks uber fun!

this_is_ameeka: Sorry I'm not there – NOT!

peterpranks: shipping you and Biebs, Ben 

(scroll down to see 67 more comments)

Chapter Five

'Here we are, gang!' announced Miss Piercy. 'And not a moment too soon. It's ten p.m. French time.'

Hermione awoke with a start at the sound of her teacher's voice. The coach still smelt faintly of vomit and her muscles ached from sitting down for so long.

'Hello, sleepyhead!' said Jessie, looking up from her console. She was covered in crisp wrappers and empty energy drink bottles.

'Have you been playing that the whole time?' said Hermione in amazement.

'Kind of,' giggled Jessie. 'I'm getting really good – I've kicked Leon's score to the kerb! Lucky I packed that spare battery pack. Wish I could keep playing . . .'

'Please put on your coats and leave the coach quietly,' said Miss Piercy, walking up and down the aisle. 'Don't forget your personal belongings and don't leave any rubbish behind. That means you, Mr Byrne!' she added playfully.

'What? I've cleared up my rubbish . . .' said Mr Byrne, looking around in a panic. 'Oh – I see, you're having me on! Ha ha!' As the joke dawned on him, his face lit up and he gazed at Miss Piercy adoringly.

'So cute,' mouthed Abby to Hermione. 'They're totally flirting!'

The coach doors opened and the teenagers jostled each other to get off the bus. The driver watched with relief as Dakota and Kayleigh (who had changed her clothes but still smelt terrible) departed.

'Look at all the snow!' gasped Abby, zipping up her jacket. 'It's crunchy too – not like the sludge we get at home.'

'And look at how high the m-mountains are . . .'

added Lucy. 'This is going to be ace!'

Hermione felt a rush of nerves now that they'd actually arrived. Looking around, she saw the dark shadows of the mountains looming over her – they were ENORMOUS!

Maybe I should have practised on a dry ski slope back home, she thought anxiously. She had a horrible feeling that her classmates would all be much better skiers than her.

'I can't wait to explore!' said Jessie, and Lucy grinned.

'Me too! This is going to b-be awesome.' They folded Hermione and Abby into a group hug and Hermione started to feel a bit better.

They all retrieved their suitcases then waited, shivering, for a few moments until a French woman came to escort them to the hotel, a short walk away.

'Kayleigh, looking forward to a shower?' asked Ben jovially.

She fixed him with a stare, scary even for her. 'GO. TO. HELL. BENJAMIN.'

Hermione and Lucy pulled 'EEK' faces at each other. It was probably for the best that they had finally arrived!

'I wonder if we'll get a curfew,' Dakota muttered to Ben, clearly feeling better. 'It looks like there are some decent bars around here.' Hermione rolled her eyes. In what world did Dakota think they would be allowed to go out drinking?

Inside the hotel, they gathered in reception, the teachers trying to chaperone them into their groups as Mr Byrne checked them all in. 'Do you think we'll have bunk beds?' asked Abby. 'If so, I'm calling the bottom one – I always worry I'm going to fall out of the top one!'

'I'm the opposite; I love the top bunk,' said Jessie. 'Makes me feel like I'm sailing a ship!'

Abby giggled. 'Well, Captain Jessie, we're a match made in heaven!'

Hermione smiled at Lucy – it would be fun sharing the other bunk with her bestie, maybe they could film each other from crazy angles.

One by one the groups went off to their rooms, calling 'see you at breakfast!' as they departed. Suddenly they were the only ones left, and Hermione became aware of a slight commotion at reception.

'Four!' Mr Byrne was saying to the receptionist. 'Quatre!' he translated.

'It's OK, *monsieur*, I can understand your English,' the woman said patiently. 'Unfortunately the final room is for three.'

He gestured at Hermione and her friends. 'But they are four! *Quatre!*' He pointed to the piece of paper in his hands. 'It was a booking for four.'

Hermione felt her stomach churn. This didn't sound good.

'I'm sorry, sir,' said the woman. 'I see now – there has been some mistake, and we are fully booked so I am afraid one of these four will have to go in another room. This one –' she pointed at Mr Byrne's list – 'this has only two occupants and it is a room for three.'

Mr Byrne glanced down. 'OK. No problem.' He turned

to face the girls, covering his mouth as he yawned deeply. 'Ladies, one of you will have to share with Dakota and Kayleigh. Any volunteers?'

The girls looked at each other in panic. 'You have GOT to be kidding me,' growled Abby.

'Is that the only room with a spare bed, sir?' asked Hermione desperately. She would rather sleep in any other room – even one with boys in it . . .

Mr Byrne sighed. 'Yes. And we'd all like to get to said beds sooner rather than later. If you can't decide between you I will make the decision for you.'

'This cannot be happening,' mumbled Hermione. There was a tense, awkward silence.

'You can see each other at breakfast,' Mr Byrne added coaxingly. 'You won't be spending much time in your rooms other than to sleep.'

'I'll do it,' said Lucy and Jessie at once. They looked at each other. 'I honestly d-don't mind,' said Lucy.

'But those guys give you such a hard time about your stammer,' said Jessie.

'Yeah, they call you Lucy Lockjaw!' added Hermione anxiously.

'I'm the one they leave alone,' continued Jessie. 'Probably cos they can tell they're no match for me.' She flexed her arm and kissed her bicep. 'And they're right!'

Mr Byrne looked faintly shocked. 'As I say, it's for sleeping arrangements only,' he spluttered.

'Plus I'm used to living with all my gross brothers, so I don't care about barf mouth Dakota,' added Jessie.

Hermione felt her heart fill with gratitude and relief. 'That's so cool of you!' she said. The others nodded, hugging Jessie. Hermione thrust the last cupcake into her hand. 'Take this – you earned it.'

Jessie grinned. 'Honestly, guys, it's no big deal.'

'Excellent,' said Mr Byrne. 'I'll take you to their room now.'

Jessie's smile faded a little and she didn't move.

Mr Byrne cleared his throat, waiting.

'Oh, you mean *now*, now?' she said. 'OK, let me get my stuff.' She slowly gathered her coat, rucksack and

suitcase then waved sadly as the teacher led her away.

'May the odds be ever in your favour,' whispered Hermione earnestly, doing the three-fingered salute from *The Hunger Games*.

'Trust you to make it about books,' said Abby, rolling her eyes.

Dear Diary,

I'm writing this by the light of my phone, under my sheets. It has been Quite A Day and now we've arrived in France at the hotel. It's freezing cold outside and there is snow everywhere. I don't know what I was expecting – it is a ski trip after all! But I guess the reality of it is just hitting me. So far I've just been having so much fun preparing for the trip. We did some awesome vlogging on the coach too and Dakota was sick *all over* Kayleigh, which was hilarious! It's like the universe is paying out revenge for all the mean stuff they've ever done to us. I actually felt a tiny bit sorry for Kayleigh who had to sit on the coach smelling terrible all day.

WORST NEWS EVER, though. There was a mix up with our rooms and Jessie is sharing with the despicable duo! She's now my ultimate hero for volunteering. The thought of spending time alone in a room with them gives me heart palpitations, but she's just a lot stronger and braver than I am, I guess, and I'm hoping they won't be totally evil to her all week. Fingers crossed she'll be able to hang out in our room most of the time anyway.

So we've got one bunk bed, which Lucy and I are sharing (I'm on the bottom) and Abby has a single bed to herself. It's a good-sized room and pretty nice. We can do some vlogging in here for sure. The others are sleeping now – Abby is snoring, ha ha! – but I'm too worried about tomorrow to sleep. Those chair lifts look terrifying – what if you slipped off them? – and the mountains are hugely steep. I keep telling myself that the ski teachers won't make us do anything too difficult on our first day, but I'm still scared to death. A small part of me (OK, not that small) wishes I'd listened to Mum and stayed behind with her and Paw Paw, but I would never admit that to anyone but you because I know it sounds pathetic.

Plus I've got my fourteenth birthday coming up which feels kind of weird because nobody knows about it! But I'm keeping it a secret as I just want to get through this week without any extra stress.

Think I'm going to read a chapter of Harry now and hopefully I'll drift off to sleep. I'll check in with you again soon, Diary, and in the meantime: WISH ME LUCK.

Hermione x

The beginners group gathered outside the ski-school building at the bottom of the slopes, chatting and sizing up the mountains around them.

'I'm so nervous,' said Hermione to Abby, wishing the others were there too. But Jessie had joined the snowboarding class, and Lucy was with the intermediate skiers. 'And I hate these boots!' They'd gone to the rental shop to hire their equipment and Hermione was finding it really hard to walk in the ugly, rigid boots. She'd already tripped over three times, the last time crashing into Dakota and earning a scowl. 'I don't think they're even the right size for me.'

'Relax, H, you'll be fine,' said Abby, removing one of her hot pink gloves to apply some suncream. 'It'll be much easier once the skis are attached.'

'*And* my arms are killing me,' Hermione added. They were holding their new skis and she was out of breath from the effort of keeping them propped up. *Why am I even here?* she asked herself grumpily. *I could be curled up at home with a good book!*

'Look, this must be our teacher!' said someone.

A young woman had walked out to greet them. '*Bonjour! Ca va, les gas?*' she asked cheerfully. Short and athletic, she looked to be in her early twenties. Her chin-length dark hair was pushed back with a sporty headband and like the other instructors she was wearing the ski school's trademark red jacket. '*Je m'appelle Astrid.*'

Sounds of confusion emanated from the group, most of whom were unfamiliar with French. 'What is she on about?' said Dakota, squinting into the sun. 'I hope she's not planning on speaking French all day!'

'She says her name is Astrid,' explained a girl in their year, Angelique, who was half French. 'She's just saying hi.'

'Hi,' mumbled most of the group, with a couple of brave '*bonjours*' thrown in too.

'It's OK – I will speak English now!' said Astrid with a grin. 'I was just giving you a taste of the beautiful French language.'

'I'm pretty sure my dad's not paying for me to have language lessons,' said Dakota sourly, tossing her hair back. Hermione cringed. How rude.

But Astrid didn't seem too bothered. She raised an eyebrow then smiled at Dakota, looking her over slowly. 'Please, what is your name?'

'Dakota,' replied Dakota archly.

'More like Puke-ota,' shouted one of the boys, hastily adding, 'Sorry,' when Dakota turned and glared at him.

'Well, Dakota,' continued Astrid. 'I'm sure your father is a very important man and I am hopeful that my teaching

will be up to his standards. Now, please remove your helmet and tie that wonderful long hair into a ponytail, so that it doesn't get in your face when you are flying down the slopes. We don't want you to risk breaking that beautiful skull of yours.'

Hermione giggled. 'I don't think Astrid is a huge fan of Dakota,' she whispered to Abby.

'Now tell me,' said the instructor, addressing the group, 'who has skied before? Anyone?'

It turned out that two members of the group had been before when they were little, and everyone else was a first timer. 'OK, so we'll start with the basics. Lesson number one, how we put our skis on!'

No going back now, thought Hermione. *Here goes nothing!*

VLOG 5

HERMIONE

(voiceover)

Bonjour! Bonjour! So we've made it to the end of a very tiring day of skiing. All that sidestepping up hills and practising the snow plough on the green slope was exhausting!

HERMIONE (CONTINUED)

(filming herself wearing jeans and a cosy white jumper)

Anyway, tonight we've got a treat and we have so earned it. We're at Maison Moustache, which is a very cute and atmospheric restaurant – and we are going to have fondue! I'm going to film a little bit for you now.

CUT TO: camera pans across a rustic French bistro with the kids sitting at long wooden tables.

ABBY

(waving at the camera)

I LOVE fondue! It's so much fun to eat and you can even get a chocolate one for dessert! Yum.

HERMIONE

So, Abs, tell us about your first day on skis?

DAKOTA

(out of shot, heard from the end of the table)

What a bunch of failures! Once again, you proved how totally uncoordinated you are.

ABBY

(loudly)

Well, I'm totally shattered and it was a lot harder than I'd expected AND my legs are killing me, but I enjoyed the hot-chocolate breaks and, of course, all the hot French ski instructors around the place . . .

Several waiters come with pots of melted cheese, which they place on hot plates. They also bring baskets of bread, potatoes and pickles to the table.

JESSIE

Let's dig in. I'm starving!

(she skewers a piece of bread with her long, thin fondue fork)

Do you just dip it in the cheese? Oops, it fell off my fork!

HERMIONE

(laughing)

I think you're meant to keep it on your fork. So, Jess, how was your lesson?

JESSIE

(chewing her cheese-dipped bread)

Snowboarding was really cool. I mean I wiped out a few times, but it was so fun. I'm excited to try some jumps tomorrow!

LUCY

You are so ace at s-sports!

JESSIE

(as another piece of bread falls into the cheese)

Better than at eating fondue! I give up! I'm gonna starve at this rate!

HERMIONE

And how did you get on, Luce?

LUCY

Pretty well . . . I was a little n-nervous at first cos I thought I'd f-forgotten how to ski, b-but I was really comfortable on the blue runs so tomorrow I might try a red one! I m-might even try skiing with a GoPro camera strapped to my h-helmet.

ERIC

Yeah, Lucy, you were really good. By tomorrow you'll be flying!

KAYLEIGH

(out of shot, heard from far end of table)

This cheese is disgusting! It's all sloppy. I want a burger and chips!

ABBY

(rolling her eyes)

Honestly, I don't know what people expect when they go abroad!

BEN

We've run out of potatoes . . . can I nick some of yours?

ABBY leans over towards the fondue pot in front of BEN and dips her fondue fork with a potato into it.

ABBY

Here!

(offers the potato to BEN)

BEN

Aw, you did it for me!

ABBY giggles flirtatiously.

DAKOTA

Eew! Ben! Germs!

HERMIONE

I'm going to wrap this up here so I can get stuck in myself. But, before I do, what's the verdict everyone? Fondue or Fon-don't?

Everyone gives a thumbs-up apart from the sulky-looking KAYLEIGH and DAKOTA.

FADE OUT.

Views: 2,789

Subscribers: 6,634

Comments:

MagicMorgan: OMG! Flirting 101! So what's up with Ben?

So-Cal-Gal: I LOVE fondue – especially the chocolate one.

Puppylove: Love love love your vlogs!

glitzygirl: So romantic! Like Lady and the Tramp! 

queen_dakota: So immature!

girlscanvlogfan: Guys, when did you hit 6,000?! Amazing!

(scroll down to see 73 more comments)

Chapter Six

Hermione's phone pinged and she sat up in her bunk to grab it.

07:02

Dad: Happy b-day, sweetheart! Hope you're having an amazing trip. Presents are waiting for when you come home . . . Dad x

07:43

Mum: Happy birthday, Hermione. Are you being careful on those slopes? Try not to eat too much cake if you celebrate later – it might give you indigestion. Paw Paw sends her love. Mum

07:44

Mum: If you do get indigestion, you can drink peppermint tea to help. Mum

Hermione grinned. Trust Mum to say something so random – she had never suffered from indigestion in her life! And her text messages always sounded so formal.

'Good morning! What are you s-smiling at?' said Lucy, dangling down from the top bunk in her cat-print onesie.

Hermione flicked her still too-short hair out of her face. 'Just my mum being weird,' she said hastily, closing the message app. She suddenly felt a pang of homesickness. Even though it was tempting to confide in the girls about her birthday she knew they wouldn't be able to keep it a secret. They'd probably force her to wear some embarrassing 'birthday girl' badge on the slopes – hashtag *awkward*!

'Mfmghghghg, why are you already awake?' croaked Abby, pulling her duvet over her head. They'd stayed up late editing their vlog after coming back from Maison Moustache the night before.

Hermione got up, pulled back Abby's duvet and thrust her alarm clock in her face. 'It's nearly eight o'clock – we're due at breakfast in twenty minutes. Then Astrid will be waiting for us after that.'

Abby groaned. 'Evil Astrid, you mean. My legs are still killing me!'

'Poor Abs!' Hermione's legs were sore too, but she felt excited about more skiing and proud of herself for surviving the first day.

There was a knock at the door and Hermione went to open it. Jessie was standing there in her ski socks and white thermals, her brother's navy salopettes folded down at the waist. 'Hiya! I managed to get out of that madhouse before the others woke up. Can I chill here while you guys get ready?'

'Sure!' said Hermione, waving her in. 'How's it going in there? We finished editing the fondue vlog last night if you want to check it out?'

Jessie nodded. 'I hate missing out on this stuff. Hi, guys!' She waved to the others and jumped on to Abby's bed. 'Get up, get up, get up!'

Abby shrieked at her to get off, but Jessie made herself comfortable against the pillows. 'So, I have gossip – kind of. Dakota and Kayleigh disappeared somewhere after dinner. I heard them creep in at like three a.m. and they're dead to the world this morning. Dakota has her sleep mask on again – it looks ridiculous!'

'More d-details, please!' said Lucy, climbing down the ladder of her bunk bed and going into the bathroom. 'It's not often we g-get the chance to infiltrate enemy ranks,' she called.

'Well, they kept bashing into things and giggling. I think they'd been drinking.' Jessie's face lit up as she remembered something. 'Ooh! Also, it turns out that Kayleigh has a little sleep-talking habit. She did it a bit on the first night, just kind of mumbling, but last night she had a full-on conversation with herself. It's just coming back to me.'

'What did she say?' asked Hermione, fascinated.

Jessie raised her eyebrow like an evil mastermind. 'The room was really quiet and I could hear practically every word.' She paused dramatically. 'Let's just say Mr Byrne came up quite a lot.'

Lucy squealed with delight in the middle of brushing her teeth.

'No way!' gasped Hermione. 'Do you think she has a crush on him?'

Jessie grinned. 'I don't know, but she kept thanking him for something and at one point she said, "chicken vindaloo, poppadoms and a plain naan, please".'

'She was ordering a takeaway in her sleep?' Abby sprang out of bed and began dancing around in her oversized Disney Princess T-shirt. 'Oh, thank you, thank you, this has made my day already!' Jessie started dancing too and they ran around the room jumping on the beds, Abby pausing to put some loud music on.

'Looks like your legs have recovered, Abs,' remarked Hermione with a smile as they all joined in the mad

dance-off. Even if they didn't know it, her friends had already given her a brilliant birthday morning.

A beautifully sunny and frosty day greeted them when their year group headed outside after breakfast. 'Aren't the mountains glorious?' said Miss Piercy happily, taking a deep breath. 'Fresh alpine air . . . what could be better!'

Mr Byrne nodded eagerly, trudging along in his eye-watering neon colours. 'Quite right, Annabel – Miss Piercy – the landscape is most stunning today.'

He didn't seem to be looking at the landscape, though, noticed Hermione. He was gazing intently at his colleague, whose cheeks had turned bright pink in the cold air. She nudged Lucy.

'It's a good thing Kayleigh is still in bed. She might be kind of jealous of the way he's checking out Miss Piercy!' Kayleigh and Dakota had both claimed they weren't feeling well and were missing out on the morning's lessons.

'Whatever,' Abby had scoffed. 'If I can show up today, with my legs, so can they.'

Lucy glanced at the teachers. 'Wow. Even Sam doesn't stare adoringly at me like that. Well, h-hardly ever!'

'Even Ron Weasley doesn't look at Hermione like that!' said Hermione, giggling.

They all boarded the little bus that took them to the slopes, then peeled off to their separate lessons. Hermione and Abby clomped over to the beginners group.

'I'm going to push you today!' announced Astrid, by way of a greeting. She surveyed the ranks of newbies before her. 'I gave you an easy start yesterday,' she continued firmly, 'but now? No more Mr Nice Guy!'

Huh? thought Hermione, looking around anxiously to see if anyone else seemed worried. What was Astrid talking about? Would they have to do those terrifying ski jumps she'd seen on TV?

But Astrid had been exaggerating. They learned a few new things, such as how to use the button lifts, which you had to squat on as they towed you up the mountain.

'These metal bars hurt my, uh, bits,' complained Eric,

triggering whoops of laughter from the group.

'I hear that a lot,' said Astrid sympathetically. 'It must be tough being a boy.'

The rest of the lesson flew by, and even Abby managed to stay upright for most of it. They took the button lifts up a small section of mountain, then dismounted, before slowly following Astrid back down in formation, winding their way down the slope and using the 'pizza slice' technique to control their speed, positioning their skis to form a triangle.

This is almost kind of fun! thought Hermione, watching the beautiful scenery pass her by as she glided along.

'Smile!' said Abby to the group, taking her phone out of her zipped pocket to film them before bumping into Ben. 'Sorry, Benjamin!' she sang as he toppled over, hands out to break his fall.

'Watch yourself, clumsy!' he said, standing up to brush himself off with a big grin on his face. 'It's true what they say – women can't drive – or ski!' He skied off before Abby could answer back.

*

There were no lessons in the afternoon so Hermione and Abby joined up with Lucy and Jessie to go skiing (and snowboarding) together. Hermione had checked with Astrid who said it was fine to go out alone, as long as they stuck to the 'green' slopes – the easiest and flattest ones, labelled green for beginners.

'My teacher told me to do the same,' said Jessie. 'I've just about got the hang of this thing.' She gestured to her board. 'I'm stacking it A LOT but it's awesome when you manage to stay up for a long run!'

They decided to try out some slopes that were further up the mountain.

'Sorry if this turns out to be really boring for you, Lucy,' said Hermione as they reached the top of a green run.

'That's OK, we t-tackled a red one this morning in our lesson,' grinned Lucy, pausing with her skis neatly parallel. 'It was super hard. I'm r-ready to take it easy now!'

'I'll stick to the sides so that you guys can ski down the

middle,' said Jessie. Boarders and skiers had different techniques, Hermione was beginning to realize – while they zigzagged across the mountain, Jessie kind of skidded down it.

'Ready, go!' cried Lucy. She swished down the mountain, followed by a wobbly Abby who seemed determined to match her friend's speed.

'WIPEOUT!' Jessie cried, falling over and spraying Hermione with snow. 'Oww!'

'You OK?' asked Hermione, looking down at her.

'My poor bum!' Jessie giggled, staying on the ground for a few seconds to get her breath back. 'Worth it, though.' She got back on her feet. 'See ya down there, H!'

Hermione watched her go, taking a minute to readjust her helmet and waiting for some other skiers to go past. Then she pushed off, gliding peacefully along, going at her own pace. *This is dreamy*, she thought, imagining Rapunzel-like hair flowing in the breeze . . . ideas for the short-story competition zooming into her head . . .

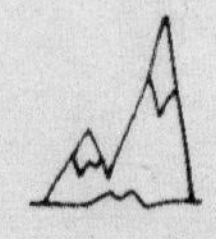

she loved the original Rapunzel but maybe it was time for a new type of fairytale heroine, one who didn't need rescuing, one who lived by her own rules, one who—

SPLAT!

'Look out!'

Before she knew it, Hermione was tumbling down the mountain, her heart in her mouth. For a few seconds she couldn't work out what was going on. Then the world stopped moving and she felt a sharp pain in her ankle.

Slowly she sat up, wincing. 'Er, wipeout?' she muttered in a daze. She looked around for a familiar face. 'Whoa!' she added, as someone skied straight past her. People were still coming down the hill and she was in their way. She tried to stand up, but pain shot up her leg and she crumpled back down again. *This is not good.* She saw that she'd lost a ski, too. 'Argh!' Another skier whooshed past her.

'Gotta get out of the way.' Hermione slowly dragged herself over to the side, panic mounting as the pain in her ankle intensified.

She got her breath back, but realized with a sinking heart that her friends wouldn't be able to see her as she was still way up the mountain and they had turned a corner on their way down. Now what? She panicked. She tried to get up again but the pain was even worse this time. Anyway, she'd lost one ski so it was hopeless. Would she have to crawl all the way down the mountain? Tears of desperation prickled in her eyes and she removed her ski goggles to wipe them away.

It's my birthday, she thought. *Why is this happening on my birthday?*

She fumbled to find her phone in her jacket pocket, but was dismayed to see that it wasn't there.

'Je peux t'aider?' said a voice. French, she thought. Through her tears she looked up to see a friendly face looming over her.

'Er – help?' she said. She gestured to her ski-less boot.

The face grinned widely below a pair of flashy reflective sunglasses. 'Ah. English? OK, that is no problem. I will speak your language. How can I help you?'

Her shoulders relaxed. So many of the French people they'd met spoke English, she thought gratefully.

'It's my ankle,' she said. 'I can't get up.' She took off her helmet before remembering about her disastrous hair situation. Too late!

But her rescuer didn't seem to notice. He took off his skis and removed his sunglasses.

'You'll be fine, don't worry,' he said reassuringly. 'What is your name?' She stared at his friendly, inquisitive eyes, a couple of shades darker than his brown skin. What was he, eighteen? Nineteen? What was he even doing on these baby slopes?

'Hermione,' she said, suddenly realizing that he was awaiting her reply.

His eyes lit up. 'Hermione,' he repeated enthusiastic-ally, squatting down beside her. 'Like the girl in Harry Potter who knows everything?'

She grinned. 'Yes.' Hermione was often asked this about her name, but she never got sick of talking about Harry Potter, and this boy obviously seemed to know his stuff. 'Although I wasn't named after her. What's yours?'

'Thierry,' he answered. '*Enchanté*.' He kissed her gloved hand like a waterproof-clad Prince Charming. 'Pleased to meet you,' he translated. He helped her get her remaining ski off, then retrieved the other one from further up the slope and clipped them together. 'Shall we try some standing, Mademoiselle Harry Potter?'

Hermione shrugged. 'OK.' She let him grab hold of her arms and lift her gently to her feet, but the pain in her ankle instantly kicked in and she winced before awkwardly sitting back down on the snow. She shivered and started to feel slightly sick.

'I don't think I can stand, let alone walk,' Hermione said, close to tears.

Thierry looked concerned. 'You're in shock from your nasty fall, I think. Here, take this.' He shrugged off his ski jacket and wrapped it around her shoulders. It smelt amazing, like eucalyptus, and the delicious heat seeped into her. 'I think there is a small chocolate bar in one of the pockets,' Thierry added. 'Please eat it, for the shock.

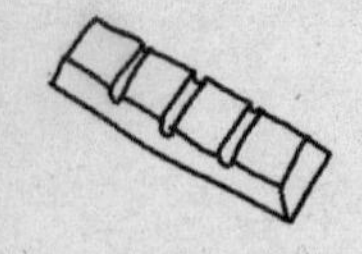

I will call for help. I have the number for emergencies – my parents made me put it in my phone!' He removed his phone from his bag and walked off to get a signal. He turned and winked. 'Stay strong, Hermione!'

Her heart leaped as she bit into the chocolate. *How nice is he?* Now that she'd had a better look at him she thought he was closer to her in age. Fifteen or sixteen, maybe? If only the others were here to help her work it out. She wondered if they'd noticed that she was missing yet.

Soon Thierry returned and kept her distracted by talking about his favourite Harry Potter storylines. Hermione was delighted to discover he'd read all the books in the series, and twenty minutes flew by, listening to his amazing English. Then a man and woman in green jackets with a white cross arrived with a stretcher on skis.

'Is that – is that for me?' she asked. It looked like something that was only brought out for serious skiing accidents.

After asking Hermione a few questions, the woman removed Thierry's jacket from her shoulders and started feeling her over for broken bones. She still felt shivery and strange and she was aware that other skiers were slowing down to look at what was going on. 'It's not often you see a stretcher on a beginner's slope,' someone commented in passing.

'Do I get a medal for that?' muttered Hermione with a sigh. 'The first person mal-coordinated enough to have an accident on a green slope?' *This is why I should never leave the house*, she thought.

'Don't listen,' said Thierry, smiling at her. 'Anyone can have a bad fall, anywhere. You were just very unlucky.'

The woman gave her a cup of hot tea from a thermos and covered her with a blanket. 'I think it is perhaps bad sprain on your ankle,' she said sympathetically. 'Try not to worry. We will take you down safely to the medical centre and from there you can call your teacher and your parents.'

'I'll follow you down,' said Thierry, putting his skis back on.

As Hermione allowed herself to be strapped into the stretcher and tucked in with cosy blankets, she looked up gratefully at her rescuer as he squeezed her hand. *Maybe it's not all bad being rescued by a fairytale prince.*

15:03

Lucy: OMG, H, where are you?

15:17

Jessie: I can't believe I left you behind, so sorry, ru OK?? xx

15:19

Abby: so worried plz call us X

VLOG 6

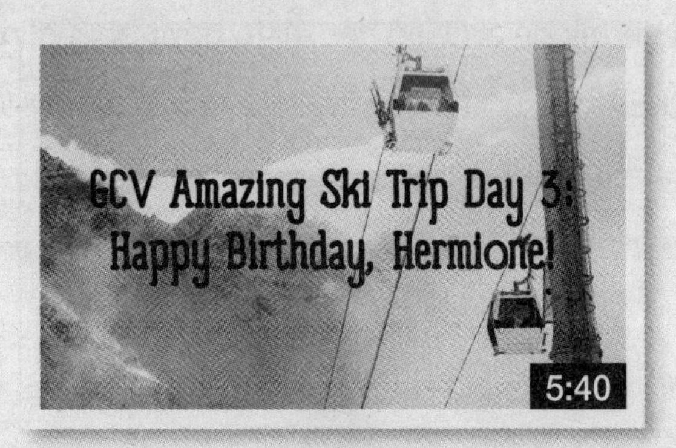

Compilation footage of JESSIE snowboarding, LUCY's view as she skis down the slopes with a GoPro strapped to her helmet, and ABBY and HERMIONE on the bunny slopes, intercut with footage of them on ski lifts, pine trees and blue sky and mountains.

ABBY

So today was a hashtag *eventful* day here on the ski trip – especially for our bestie Hermione! She took a spill on the slopes and was carted off to the medical centre on a stretcher. When she finally got back to our hotel . . .

Guess what?

CUT TO: LUCY, HERMIONE and ABBY's hotel room – in darkness.

Lots of voices shout: 'SURPRISE! SURPRISE!' and start singing 'Happy Birthday'. Lights switch on, revealing a hotel room decorated with banners, streamers and balloons.

Camera turns to HERMIONE in open doorway, on crutches, with MISS PIERCY behind her. HERMIONE is open-mouthed in amazement. LUCY rushes up to HERMIONE and gives her a hug.

LUCY

Oh, H, what a c-crazy thing to happen on your birthday!

HERMIONE

My birthday. How did you know? I thought I'd kept it a secret . . .

JESSIE

(from behind the camera)

You should know you can't keep a secret from us!

LUCY

Don't you remember the vlog we did about our birthdays and star signs?

(taps her own head)

Everything g-gets filed away in here!

HERMIONE

(laughing)

That was ages ago!

ABBY

We brought all the party stuff from home – apart from the cake and snacks. Of course, the cake won't be as delicious as one you could bake.

MISS PIERCY

Let Hermione sit down, poor thing, I'm sure she's still in shock. Hermione, remember you need to keep your leg propped up on some pillows and do try to get some sleep. Lucy, please look after her. And happy birthday, Hermione! Behave yourselves, everyone.

(she leaves the room)

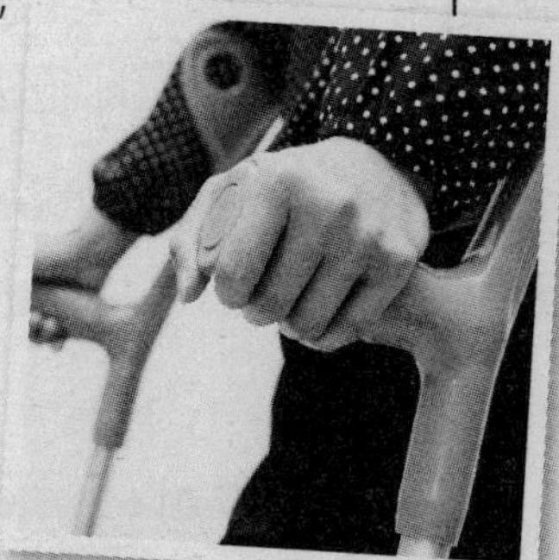

LUCY

Are you OK, H?

HERMIONE

(welling up)

I'm just stunned – and really touched. You know I don't like to make a fuss, but this . . .

(she waves her hand at the banners and balloons)

has made me so happy . . .

JESSIE

Are you hungry? Have you eaten anything since lunch?

You must be starving! Well, anyway, I am . . .

where are the snacks, guys?

Bags of crisps, other snacks, sweets and bottles of Coke are passed around and eaten and drunk noisily.

ABBY

So, H, tell us everything! I hear you were hashtag *rescued* by a gorgeous French boy!

JESSIE

(eagerly)

Are you going to see him again?

HERMIONE

Probably not. He was just a really kind person who was unlucky enough to stumble across me – almost literally.

LUCY

And how is your f-foot? Does it hurt?

HERMIONE

(with a sigh)

Apparently, I've sprained my ankle. It's not broken so I won't need a cast, but I've got a bandage and I'm not allowed to put weight on it for a few weeks – maybe even a month. Plus I have crutches.

JESSIE

So no more skiing for you, then! What are you going to do all day?

HERMIONE

Luckily I brought some books – plus I've got something I need to write, and I'll be able to do some extra stuff for the vlog!

LUCY and ABBY who have been fussing over something in the background appear with a three-tier cake with lit candles and sing 'Happy Birthday'.

HERMIONE (CONTINUED)

Guys! Thank you . . . this is a birthday I'll never forget.

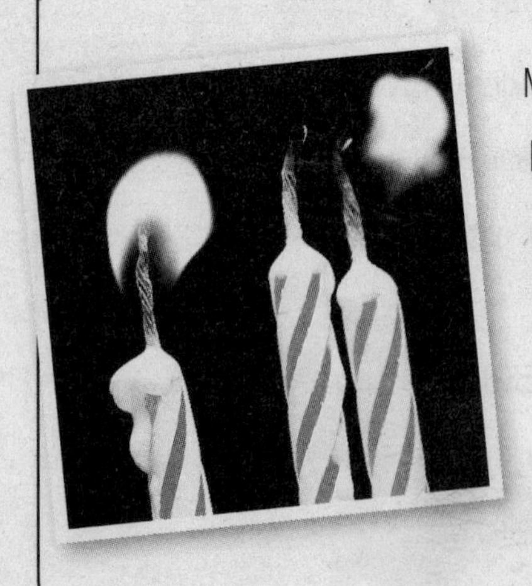

Montage of HERMIONE blowing out her candles, cutting an enormous slice of cake and being hugged by all the girls, before JESSIE wraps her up in one of the birthday banners . . .

FADE OUT.

Views: 2,705

Subscriptions: 6,939

Comments:

MagicMorgan: Happy birthday, H! So unlucky spraining your ankle. ☹

Xxrainbowxx: Love surprise parties! Had one for my 13th.

queen_dakota: Desperate. Attention-seeking.

StephSaysHi: such a thoughtful idea! #friendshipgoals

StalkerGurl: No boys?! ☹

SassySays: Happy birthday, Hermione ❤❤❤

my_cute_bookshelf: Hope you get some cool new books for your birthday! #bookhaul vlog if you do!

(scroll down to see 51 more comments)

Chapter Seven

The next morning Lucy helped Hermione down to breakfast, while Abby went to knock for Jessie. It had taken Hermione a few seconds to remember her injury when she'd woken up, and now she felt self-conscious and awkward walking around with her new crutches.

'I'll get you what you n-need from the buffet,' offered Lucy, helping her sit down at a table and bringing another chair for her to prop up her leg. 'What would you like?' she asked. 'Now that your Pr-Prince Charming isn't here, you'll have to rely on me to help you out.'

Hermione laughed. 'A croissant and an orange juice please.' Deep down she was feeling slightly sad that

the excitement of yesterday was over. Her surprise party had been so much fun – plus the big rescue! But after telling her friends all about Thierry she'd suddenly realized she would never see him again, and now she'd have to spend the rest of the trip resting her ankle in the hotel while her friends were having fun on the slopes. She'd refused her mum's offer to fly out and bring her home early when they'd had a phone call in the medical centre. At least she could finish her Rapunzel story – the deadline was tomorrow.

'Something's kicking off,' said Abby excitedly, joining her at the table. She lowered her voice. 'Miss Piercy is outside with a face like thunder, making calls. I heard something about a final straw. She looks FURIOUS!'

Hermione wrinkled her brow. 'Weird – I wonder what that's about. Did you find Jessie?'

Abby shook her head. 'That's the other thing. Nobody answered the door so I assumed they were already at breakfast. But I can't see them in here,' she said, looking around. 'I'll message her.' She pulled out her phone, but

then Hermione stopped her and frantically gestured to the buffet where Miss Piercy and Mr Byrne were standing next to an annoyed-looking Dakota and Kayleigh and a tearful Jessie.

Lucy rushed back to the table, an anxious look on her face.

'Is everyone here?' asked Miss Piercy. She did a quick headcount of the breakfasting students. 'Right, well, I'm afraid that we have rather an unfortunate announcement to make before you can get on with your day.'

Dakota rolled her eyes as Jessie gazed despondently at her friends. Abby mouthed something at her and she shrugged sadly.

What on earth's happened? thought Hermione, feeling sick. Jessie looked completely shell-shocked.

'Late last night, these three girls were found in a local bar after curfew,' began Miss Piercy.

'Party!' someone whooped. Mr Byrne glared at the pupil responsible disapprovingly.

Miss Piercy took a deep breath and continued. Hermione had never seen their usually sweet-tempered teacher so angry. 'This in itself is completely irresponsible behaviour, of course, but what is more – the girls were all caught with alcohol – which, may I remind you, is strictly against the rules of this school *and* against the law. Their actions were stupid and dangerous, and I dare say the girls aren't feeling too clever this morning.'

'I feel fine,' muttered Kayleigh, although the bags under her eyes and her green-tinged skin told a different story. 'Top of the world, might go for a jog, actually.' There was a smattering of giggles.

'That is ENOUGH, Kayleigh,' snapped Miss Piercy. She sighed. 'As a result of this disappointing behaviour, the girls' parents have been called and we are arranging an early departure home for them.'

'What?' cried Abby. 'They can't leave – we've still got three days to go.'

Mr Byrne stepped in. 'Well, they should have thought about that before making the decision to act so stupidly. We can't allow them to remain here now that they have put themselves at risk and broken the school's regulations about alcohol, not to mention the law. Everyone knows the rules and this puts the school's reputation in jeopardy. What would prospective parents think?'

Never mind prospective parents, thought Hermione. *If my mum knew about this, I'd be on my way home faster than Harry on his Firebolt.*

'They'd probably think "awesome, what a fun school"!' called Ben, raising a grin from Eric. Then he seemed to lose his nerve. 'Just kidding, sir.'

Hermione looked at Jessie in confusion, then at Lucy and Abby, who seemed similarly baffled. Jessie had told them about Dakota and Kayleigh sneaking out after curfew earlier in the week, but surely she wouldn't have joined them? She'd spent most of the time trying to avoid their company. This didn't make any sense.

'A cab is coming to take them to the airport shortly,' continued Mr Byrne. There was a big gasp as the reality of the situation hit home. 'Their parents have had to pay for last-minute plane tickets. Unfortunately Ms Hawken will also have her trip cut short as she has kindly volunteered to escort them back to the UK.'

Jessie hung her head. Hermione had never seen her this quiet. She couldn't imagine the amount of trouble her friend would get into when she got back to the UK.

'OK, everyone. I hope that's given you a very clear message to be on your best behaviour for the remainder of this trip,' said Miss Piercy. 'Go back to your breakfasts. You three, you should eat something before the taxi comes.'

Jessie still looked shell-shocked as Lucy and Abby went up to her and hugged her.

'C-come and sit with us,' said Lucy. 'And tell us w-what the hell is going on!'

Jessie selected a pain au chocolat and joined them at the table. 'My last French pastry,' she said, picking at it sadly. There was a brief pause as they all looked at each other, waiting for her to say something.

'SO?' said Abby finally, unable to contain herself. 'What happened? Spill!'

'It's a really long story. I'll message you guys later, but in a nutshell yours truly, massive idiot that I am, went to the bar that I knew they'd gone to, to warn them that Mr Byrne was doing bed checks after curfew. I knew the bar was right next door to the hotel so I popped in to warn them.'

'But why?' asked Hermione, totally bemused. Dakota and Kayleigh never had a thought for anyone else; they didn't deserve a warning. She glanced over at them. Dakota was frowning into a bowl of fruit and yoghurt and Kayleigh had her head on the table, while some of their hangers-on muttered that the whole thing was outrageous.

'I didn't want to deal with them getting punished and being in a foul mood,' Jessie explained. 'And I thought maybe, if I did something nice for them, we could start to build some bridges.'

'Oh, Jess, y-you're so sweet,' said Lucy.

'And dumb,' added Abby, rolling her eyes. 'Too trusting! How are we meant to finish our vlogging without you?'

'So what actually happened?' asked Hermione, elbowing Abby aside. 'Give us the details.'

Jessie shrugged. 'Abby's right. I'm an idiot. When I got to the bar, I found them flirting with these boys from a French school and trying to get them to buy them drinks cos they knew they wouldn't get served. The boys didn't really want to, but then eventually they bought a round of shots. Dakota didn't care about the bed checks even though I was begging them to hurry up and leave. I should've just left them to it . . . but I stayed around, and one of them handed me a shot. Which was EXACTLY the moment Miss Piercy and Ms Hawken walked into the bar and caught us red handed.'

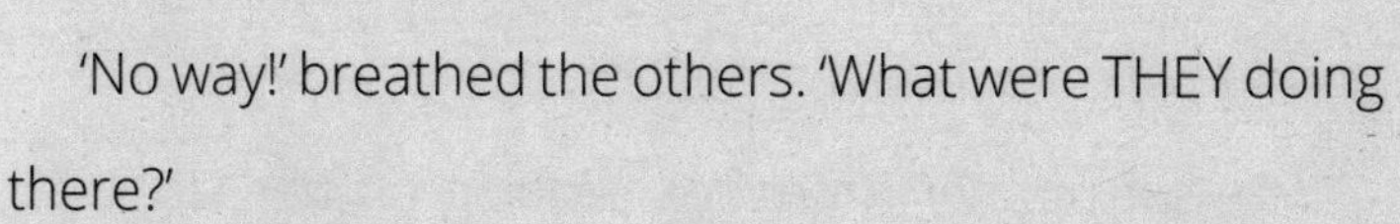

'No way!' breathed the others. 'What were THEY doing there?'

'Who knows. Maybe they just wanted a drink. Or maybe the barman called the hotel to report us. He did ask me where we were staying, but I thought he was just being chatty. Anyway, they *freaked out*, obviously, and it all went downhill from there. They didn't seem interested in hearing my side of the story. I didn't even drink the shot – much less want it! It's so unfair!'

'I'm going to speak to the teachers about this,' said Abby determinedly, getting up from the table. 'This is not OK.'

But then Miss Piercy shouted, 'Taxi's here!' and Jessie was whisked away from them by Ms Hawken before they could do a single thing about it.

I can't even message her, thought Hermione, *that stupid phone of mine is still somewhere on the mountain.*

DRING! DRING!

The hotel room landline woke Hermione, who had nodded off over her competition entry.

She sat up, her notebook slipping off her lap, then reached for the handset. 'Hello?'

'*Bonjour*? Room three-six-seven?'

'Yes?' she said hesitantly.

'There is a visitor for you in reception. You are Miss Chan, yes? With the bad ankle?'

'Er . . . yes.'

'Shall I send them up?'

'Who—' The dialling tone cut her off. *Who can it be?* thought Hermione. Was it Jessie? Had she somehow convinced Ms Hawken to let her come back?

A few moments later there was a knock at her door and she called, 'Come in!'

'*Bonjour*, Mademoiselle Harry Potter!'

'Thierry! What are you doing here?' It was weird seeing him in regular clothes. He was wearing skinny jeans and a soft grey jumper plus some red – and soggy – Converse All-Stars.

'Well, first of all, I thought perhaps you'd like this back –' he handed Hermione her phone, causing a yelp of delight – 'and, secondly, I heard there was a party and I was not invited?'

'What? I, er, it was my birthday and I – it was a surprise,' spluttered Hermione. 'Oh, you're winding me up!'

He looked around at the cards and banners, and smiled. 'Yes. There were a few clues around. So when *was* it your birthday?' he asked, sitting down.

'Yesterday, in fact,' she said shyly. 'My friends did all this to cheer me up after my accident. Where did you find my phone?'

'I found it on the mountain when I retrieved your ski, then I put it in my pocket for safe-keeping and completely forgot about it with all the dramatics. When I found it this morning, I called the first number on your recently called list, which was an Abby, and she told me the name of your hotel.'

'Wow, thanks,' said Hermione. 'I've been lost without it and it has so many notes on it, of books I want to read and stuff.'

'You really love the books,' he said, glancing at her bunk bed, which was covered with paperbacks. 'All this for a week's holiday?'

'Yeah well . . .' She blushed. 'Just as well now that I've got all this free time on my hands. Although I should

also do some vlogging now that Jessie's gone home. We have this rota, you see . . .' Before she knew it, she was babbling away about Girls Can Vlog and their goals for the channel.

'Anyway, I'm taking up your time,' she said, suddenly realizing that Thierry hadn't spoken in a while. 'I bet you're dying to hit those slopes again!'

He cleared his throat. 'Actually, not so much.' He picked up a copy of *The Hobbit* and glanced it over. 'My family, they love the skiing. They encourage me to enjoy it too when we come on holiday every year. But me – I would rather be like you, indoors and with a good book!'

Hermione's heart skipped a beat. 'Really?' she asked.

'Yes, of course!' He sat down cross-legged on the opposite bed. 'So tell me more about this vlogging. Can I help?'

11.29

Hermione: Finally got my phone back – are you OK?

11.30

Jessie: SAVE ME

11.31

Hermione: ??

11.33

Jessie: At the airport. Dakota puked twice on the way here and is now going on about Ben . . .

11.35

Hermione: Why?

11.36

Jessie: Apparently he's not texting her or liking any of her selfies.

11.37

Hermione: Maybe not too happy about her flirting with those guys in the bar?

11.39

Jessie: Maybe – anyway she won't stop talking! And Mum keeps sending me evil messages – I am in the BIGGEST trouble.

11.40

Hermione: You poor thing, so not your fault. We miss you!!

11.41

Jessie: I miss you 2. Boohoo ☹

11.44

Hermione: ☺ Guess what? I'm about to film a vlog with a BOY.

11.45

Jessie: Whaaat? Who?

11.50

Hermione: Wait and see! xxx

VLOG 7

FADE IN: DAYTIME IN THE HOTEL LOUNGE. HERMIONE and THIERRY are sitting on a sofa together.

HERMIONE

Hello, or should I say *bonjour* as we are still in France on the ski trip. And I am STILL no longer able to ski.

(points to her foot propped up on a chair with pillows)

But the good news is that I'm with my new friend Thierry!

(gestures shyly to Thierry)

THIERRY

(with a little wave)

Bonjour! It is my first time vlogging on YouTube. I have – how you say – a few nerves.

HERMIONE

Trust me, if I can do it, anyone can!

(she turns back to the camera)

Me and Thierry are both massive bookworms so we thought we'd just have a chilled-out conversation about reading. So, Thierry, we realized early on that we both love Harry Potter. What is your favourite book in the series?

THIERRY

Let me think . . . for me it is *Harry Potter et les Reliques de la Mort* or, I think, *Harry Potter and the Deathly Hallows* in English. The last one. It is so epic, with the ultimate battle between good versus evil. I was so emotional the first time I read it and found out how the series ended.

HERMIONE

No spoilers, for anyone who hasn't read it or watched the movies yet!

THIERRY mimes zipping his mouth.

THIERRY

And your favourite?

HERMIONE

It's so difficult . . . I love them all, but it's probably *Harry Potter and the Prisoner of Azkaban* – when Harry has to start defending himself against the Dementors. Ooh, and I love the bit where he finds out the truth about Sirius.

(THIERRY nods eagerly)

Again, I'll avoid spoilers! So, next question, if you were at Hogwarts, which house would you want to be sorted into by the Sorting Hat?

(she smiles at the camera)

We've all thought about this, right, guys?

THIERRY

Of course, I am a Ravenclaw, the most unique house! And you? Are you a Gryffindor like the other Hermione?

HERMIONE

(beaming)

No – not brave enough. But how amazing is that, because I'd be a Ravenclaw too. They're the most creative. Even if it's extra tricky to get into their common room, ha ha! All hail Rowena Ravenclaw!

THIERRY

I hope we can be on the Quidditch team together . . .

HERMIONE

(laughing)

Me too! OK, next we wanted to talk a bit about our reading habits and quirks. Firstly, where is your favourite place to read?

THIERRY

Mostly, when I am travelling on the metro. The underground. Or if I am in bed on the weekends I will stay many hours with a good book! I have the perfect pillow to lean on.

HERMIONE

(face lighting up)

Same here! I also love to read in the bath . . . Sometimes when I get lost in a book the water gets cold and my fingers and toes have turned into prunes and
I haven't even noticed.

(pause)

Not that I'm always naked when I'm reading!
Er . . . mostly I have clothes on.

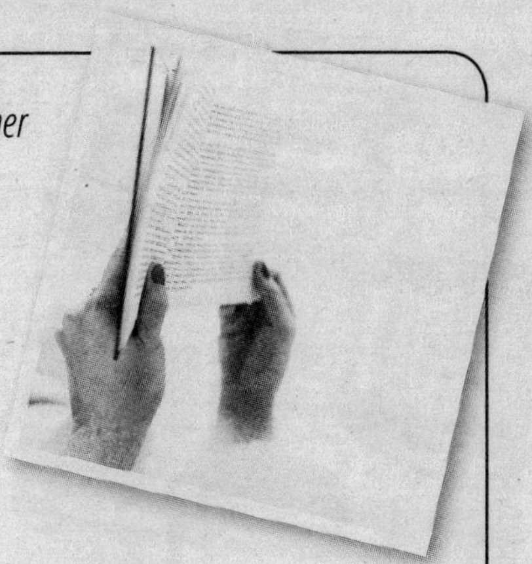

(flustered, she looks down at her notebook)

THIERRY

(grinning)

You are so funny! I too like to read with my clothes on. Next question?

HERMIONE

Which type of book do you like? Real, or ebook?

THIERRY

I don't like the ebook – I love the smell of paper. Mainly I choose a paperback so I can carry it around. Also I like to listen to an audio book sometimes when I am jogging. You?

HERMIONE

I love paperbacks too, but I collect hardback editions of my favourite novels for my bookcases. I have two sets of Harry Potter –

the hardbacks, which I try to keep pristine, and the paperbacks, which are battered to death! No ebooks for me. I can't bear the thought of running out of battery at a really important bit in the story!

THIERRY

And you'd maybe drop them in the bath.

HERMIONE

Ha ha, true . . . so, do you read one book at a time, or do you alternate?

THIERRY

Me, I like to always have one fiction book and one non-fiction on the go at the same time. Sometimes a graphic novel too.

HERMIONE

Interesting, I only read one book at a time and, no matter where I am or what I'm doing, I can't put my book down unless I've got to the end of a chapter.

THIERRY

(grinning)

This also explains the prune toes, eh?

HERMIONE

Enough about the bath already! So I think it's time to wrap up this video and to give a big *merci* to Thierry for joining in.

THIERRY

Well, thank you for inviting me. It was a pleasure.

HERMIONE

If you enjoyed the video, be sure to give us a thumbs-up and don't forget to let us know about your Harry Potter allegiances down below.

HERMIONE and THIERRY

Au revoir!

FADE OUT.

Views: 2,589

Subscriptions: 7,201

Comments:

HPsuperfan: Woohoo! I'm Ravenclaw too! The best!

my_cute_bookshelf: Hufflepuff over here. And paperbacks all the way – though Kindles are good for holidays.

pink_sprinkles: Shipping you 2 bookworms! 

NevilleLongbottomFanClub: #Gryffindor

PrankingsteinCharlie: I'm just a muggle lol

ShyGirl1: I did a quiz and got Slytherin . . . What

went wrong? Help!

peterpranks: I thought this was a ski trip?

Cobra1: Do they deliver Chinese takeaway to Hogwarts, Hermione? Don't forget your chopsticks!

MagicMorgan [reply to Cobra1]**:** Slytherin serpent over here? Weird comment . . .

(scroll down to see 45 more comments)

Chapter Eight

10:44

Mum: How are you, Hermione? Are you resting your ankle properly?

10:45

Hermione: Yes, no need to worry :)

10:46

Mum: If you don't rest it, it will take longer to heal you know.

10:47

Hermione: I know, Mum!!! How are you?

10:48

Mum: I miss you. X

10:49

Hermione: Mum, that's the first text kiss you've ever sent. I'm so proud!! Xx

10:55

Mum: You know, I'm not a bad person.

10:56

Hermione: What? Of course not?!

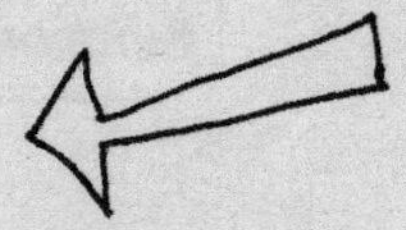

10:58

Mum: With the divorce . . . I hope you understand.

10:59

Hermione: Understand what?

11:00

Mum: It wasn't all me. Your father made some bad choices.

11:01

Hermione: ???

11:05

Mum: Anyway, talk to you later, Hermione. Rest your leg.

11:06

Hermione: Wait, what did you mean? About Dad.

11:09

Mum: It doesn't matter. You can talk to your father when you get back.

11:12

Hermione: OK. I'm really, really sorry I said that thing about you driving Dad away. I didn't mean it xx

11:13

Mum: I know. Goodbye, Hermione. X

It was mid-morning and the others were all at ski school. Hermione was sitting on her bed, rereading the odd text conversation she'd just had with her mum. It was one of the nicest chats she'd had with her in ages, but it had left her wondering . . . What HAD the divorce been about? She still didn't know, and while she'd thought it had to do with her mum's nagging and strict ways, now she wondered if there was more to it. She sent another message.

11:32

Hermione: Mum, were you trying to tell me something?? I can't read your mind . . . x

She watched her phone for a few moments. No reply. *Guess I'll have to speak to Dad.* She sighed. This was so frustrating!

To cheer herself up, she hopped over to Abby's laptop and started scrolling through the comments

on the Ravenclaw video. She was excited to see what people would say about it – she knew reading was nerdy to some people, but she wanted to share her love of books. Every time she met someone who didn't read for pleasure, she felt sorry for them because they didn't realize what amazingness they were missing out on.

She was thrilled to see that loads of viewers had responded positively to the video. That would show Abby, who sometimes worried that book vlogs were boring and might put off their subscribers. Thierry and his razor-sharp cheekbones had probably helped! Then she gasped, noticing a horrible comment, which made fun of her ethnicity. Something about chopsticks and takeaways . . . *What on earth?*

Loads of people including Morgan had fought back, but it really stung. It wasn't the usual Dakota rubbish, but something more basic and mindless. Racism.

I guess trolling is part of the deal when your numbers start to grow, Hermione thought, *but why do some people have to be so nasty?* For some reason the negative comments always stuck in her head for a longer time than the positive ones. She deleted the comment, blocked the user and tried not to think any more about it.

She finished editing her competition entry, in which Rapunzel had a short bob and ended up rescuing the long-haired prince from the tower. She smiled to herself as she typed it up on Abby's computer and emailed it off. Then she started mulling over the hateful comment again, and to avoid obsessing about it she went downstairs and managed to set herself up in the bar area of the hotel, with some assistance from a waiter who helped her prop up her leg on a chair and brought her a hot chocolate.

As she opened her book she heard a familiar voice. 'Ah, there she is! Mademoiselle Harry Potter!' She looked up in surprise at Thierry, strolling in through reception. 'Are we viral sensations yet?'

She grinned. 'Thierry, hi!' She'd exchanged numbers with him yesterday after the vlog, but hadn't really expected to see him again. Definitely not this soon. 'You really don't like skiing, do you?' she joked. He ordered a cafe au lait, then sat down next to her. *He's so gorgeous*, she remembered with a shock as he took off his jacket and elegantly crossed his legs. Today he was wearing a stylish cable-knit cream jumper and she suddenly regretted her comfy jogging bottoms and sweatshirt.

He tossed a package on to the table. 'I'm sorry it's late, but how do you say, better late than never, eh?'

He got me a birthday present! squealed Hermione to herself as she checked out the cute red-and-white check wrapping paper. Today was looking up.

'What's this?' she asked, playing dumb. This was a big moment, the first time a boy had ever given her a present, but Thierry couldn't know that. The waiter, who was clearing a table behind Thierry, caught her eye and winked.

'For your birthday,' Thierry said with a shrug. 'I saw it and I thought you might like it.'

'This is so nice of you!' she said shyly, leaning forward to pick up the package. Slowly she unwrapped it, taking care not to rip the paper. Her hands were shaking a

little. *Be cool, Hermione,* she told herself. *For all he knows, you get presents from boys on a weekly basis.*

The waiter brought over Thierry's coffee, lingering for a few seconds to see her open the gift.

A brightly coloured paperback fell into her lap. *Harry Potter à L'École des Sorciers* read the cover. 'OK, so I can work out the first bit of that title,' she giggled. 'Help me out with the rest?'

'It translates as "Harry Potter and the school for wizards",' explained Thierry. 'It's the first one in the series – which you know as *Harry Potter and the Philosopher's Stone*, right?' He sipped his coffee.

'Right. So cool,' gasped Hermione. 'Until we filmed our video, I hadn't thought about the books having different titles all over the world!' She looked up from the book, her eyes shining. 'Thank you so much, Thierry. This is great.'

'No problem,' he said. 'I thought maybe it would inspire you to read in French. I am sure you know the story off by heart so perhaps it won't be too difficult to figure out the vocabulary.'

She nodded fervently. 'It's so thoughtful of you. I can't wait to get stuck in!' Not only was this the first present she'd received from a boy, it was the best present she'd ever had.

Thierry drained his coffee. 'Anyway, I'm afraid I must go to meet my father.'

'Now?' she asked, still clutching the book.

'Yes, unfortunately I promised I would do some skiing with him this morning.' He pulled a face. 'Poor me! It was nice to see you, Hermione.'

A few moments later he was off, leaving her with a big goofy smile on her face.

What just happened? she thought in a daze.

'Moi, je suis Gryffindor,' added the waiter, clearing away Thierry's cup.

12:21

Hermione: Thanks again for my amazing present :) xx

12:25

Thierry: No problem. Enjoy!

12:26

Hermione: *J'adore* Harry! Xx

12:27

Hermione: Let me know if you want to hang out again? xx

12:28

Hermione: Ravenclaw forever xx

12:30

Hermione: Lucy! Thierry brought me a book to the hotel!! Harry Potter in French!

12:31

Lucy: No way!

12:32

Hermione: He said it would 'inspire me to learn French' ❤❤❤

12:34

Lucy: LOL maybe he wants you to move here!

12:35

Lucy: Ooh la la, Hermione has a French boyfriend!!

'I need an afternoon off skiing,' announced Abby at lunch, an hour later. The girls had crowded round what had become 'their' table in the hotel restaurant. 'The blister on my right foot is getting worse and I'm in sooo much pain.' She took off her boot and rubbed her foot. 'H, do you want to hang out after this?'

'Er, yes!' said Hermione. 'The hotel loner over here would love some company. If you're sure?'

'Very sure,' groaned Abby, hastily putting her sweaty sock away as Ben walked past. 'Honestly, who invented this sport? It's hashtag *torture*! I'd rather sit through double English.'

'That bad, hey?' remarked Miss Piercy from a neighbouring table, before hungrily tucking into a burger.

The girls giggled. *Oops!* mouthed Abby to her friends. 'No offence, miss,' she said quickly. 'I actually meant – er – your English lessons are really fun. Like, MORE fun than skiing. Which is MASSIVELY fun.'

Hermione shook her head and Lucy grinned. 'I'll g-get you some blister plasters later, Abs. I've got loads in the room.'

Abby nodded gratefully. 'Honestly, my feet are in shreds! Sorry if that's TMI . . .'

'First me, then Jessie, now you – we're dropping like flies.' Hermione took out her phone and angled it at her and Abby. 'Injury selfie!'

'Injury selfie,' chorused Abby, posing with a 'poor me' expression. She turned to Hermione. 'I know, why don't we check out that pancake place in the ski village later?'

'Oh my gosh, yes!' cried Hermione. 'I'm getting better on my crutches and I seriously need to get out of this hotel.' She had started feeling stir crazy and since Thierry had left that morning she had alternated between checking her phone for messages and rewatching their

vlog, obsessing over his beautiful face and voice. *Not healthy . . .*

'Great, we can take the bus there after lunch. As long as you don't mind being abandoned, Luce?' said Abby. 'It's probably for the best. I feel like I'm holding you back when we ski together – you're so fast!'

Lucy grinned. 'I'll be fine, I'll join a group with s-some people from my class.' She turned her glance to Hermione. 'No giving Abby any Thierry g-gossip without me, OK? This adorable book nerd romance has me h-hooked!'

Hermione coughed. 'There's nothing more to tell,' she said briskly. 'He hasn't replied to my last message anyway.' She had a sinking feeling that she should have played it cooler. Maybe she shouldn't have sent him so many texts. And why oh why had she mentioned her prune toes in the video?

'He hasn't replied YET!' said Abby, her eyes lighting up. 'These French men, they play by their own rules. Give him time . . .'

*

Hermione still hadn't received a reply a couple of hours later as she and Abby decided to have a second pancake at the crêperie. She ordered the same again – Nutella and banana.

'Lemon and sugar for *moi*!' said Abby to their waitress. '*Merci!* So anyway, H, I've decided I'm definitely over Charlie.' She'd finally opened up to Hermione about her boy drama and at the rate she was talking it seemed as if she had a lot to get off her chest. Which was fine by Hermione as it kept her from checking her phone. Plus she was fascinated by Abby's dilemma.

'Why, what's Charlie done now?' she asked. Abby and Charlie had kissed a few times and spent quite a lot of time together before Christmas, but they hadn't seen much of each other since. Hermione had a secret theory that Charlie liked Abby a lot, but was scared of getting rejected by his best friend's little sister.

'He's been texting me hashtag *advice*.' Abby showed Hermione the messages. 'His messages go on a bit, but basically he says that I should be careful of Ben,' she said, rolling her eyes. 'Charlie watched our vlog in the fondue restaurant and said I was acting really flirty around him.'

Hermione giggled. 'Well, he's not wrong about that!'

Abby looked appalled. 'I do not act flirty around Ben! Do I?'

'You just seem . . . a little sparklier than your usual sparkly self when he's in the room,' said Hermione tactfully. 'Especially now that Dakota's not here. And Charlie's obviously got a bit jealous.'

'It's so annoying,' said Abby. 'Messaging me to say I should be "careful" is over the top, don't you think? Just because Ben was a bit of an idiot last term, it doesn't mean we can't still hang out. He's with Dakota anyway so it's not like anything's going to happen. Besides, Charlie's not even my boyfriend. He can't tell me what to do.'

'Mmm,' said Hermione in a non-committal tone. She knew what Charlie meant. Even if Abby was downplaying it now, Ben had really upset her few months ago by giving her mixed messages. And Hermione wasn't convinced that Bakota was much of a thing any more.

'Yum!' said Abby, taking a photo of her pancake as it was placed in front of her. 'Serious pancake goals. The food on this trip has been incredible.'

Hermione picked up her phone to do the same and, without properly meaning to, checked for a new message. Nothing. Her heart sank.

'And, anyway, so what if I think Ben is fun to be around,' continued Abby, gesturing with her knife and fork. 'Yes, he's kind of cute, I said it. Ooh!' she looked out of the window. 'Speaking of which – isn't that . . . Thierry?' She peered out at the people who were taking their skis off outside the little strip of restaurants and bars.

'What?!' said Hermione.

'It *is* him. I recognize him from your vlog!' said Abby gleefully. 'HEY, THIERRY!' She knocked on the glass, waving madly and pointing to Hermione's head. 'Your new friend is here!'

Hermione covered her face as Thierry looked

over in surprise, then waved.

'COME IN, COME IN!' yelled Abby, causing the other people in the restaurant to turn and stare. 'Yes, he's coming! I can't believe I finally get to meet him.'

This is so humiliating, Hermione thought. *He probably thinks I'm stalking him because he didn't text me back.*

'Do NOT embarrass me,' she said to Abby. She pushed her plate away, her appetite suddenly gone. 'Promise me? Oh my God, here he comes.'

'Here, borrow my lipgloss,' said Abby quickly, but Hermione was fraught with nerves and shook her head. Instead she concentrated on trying to fix her stupid hair.

'Hello, girls. Hello again, Hermione,' said Thierry a few moments later. 'Wow! These crêpes look delicious.'

'They are! Hi, I'm Abby – we spoke on the phone that time,' jumped in Abby. 'You were amazing on the book vlog. Do you think you'll do any more booktuber stuff in the future? Plus it was so sweet of you to get Hermione that French Harry Potter. Wasn't it, H?'

'Uh, yes. Really nice,' mumbled Hermione, mentally begging Abby to stop talking. Thierry looked slightly taken aback by Abby's enthusiasm.

'When she first showed it to me I thought it was a Valentine's Day present, ha ha, as you know the big day is tomorrow!' said Abby happily. 'Then I remembered it had been her birthday this week.'

'ABBY,' said Hermione in a panic as Thierry began to look more and more uncomfortable. Why was she talking about Valentine's Day of all things? 'Thierry probably has to be on his way. And we need to get the bill.'

'Huh? Why?' asked Abby, looking confused. 'There's no rush, is there? Wait, I'll go. Leave you two to it. I'm sure there are some new books you'd lurrrve to discuss!' She winked at Hermione.

Thierry cleared his throat. 'You girls stay here and enjoy your crêpes. I'm afraid I do have to go,' he said slowly. 'I'm meeting my friend Louis at the cafe next door.' Hermione's heart fell; it was clear he was desperate to leave. 'It was fun to bump into you! Enjoy the rest of your trip.' He did a cute goodbye wave and trudged off noisily in his ski boots.

'He seems so nice!' said Abby, tucking into her pancake again. 'And he's hot. Lucy's going to be gutted that she missed him.' But Hermione's eyes were welling up with tears. Thierry had made it very clear – he wasn't interested. And a few minutes later, a text on her phone confirmed it.

16:03

Thierry: I hope I didn't give you the wrong idea. Can we be friends? :) Thierry

Dear Diary,

We have to film some stupid Valentine's vlog in a minute but I had to get some stuff off my chest first. It's been a truly terrible day.

In no particular order, because EVERYTHING is a mess and I don't know which bits are worse – Thierry rejected me after we did an amazing vlog together. I can't believe I thought he liked me, just because he bought me a book . . . Why do I always kid myself that I live in this fantasy land where everything is perfect? Then Mum sent me a weird message about the divorce, which has made me wonder a million different things. It's so confusing when you're used to your parents being a single unit and then suddenly they hate each other and you have to talk to them separately – arghhhh! So I have to talk to Dad, which I'm dreading. Like, what happened??? On top of this someone left a really stupid, hurtful, RACIST comment on the vlog and so I have to live with knowing there is someone out there who hates me for no reason.

I wish I could curl up with a book, but now I have to go and talk about stupid romance.

This is the worst day of my life.

Hermione x

VLOG 8

Night-time. ABBY, HERMIONE and LUCY sitting in their room around a table to which they have tied heart-shaped balloons.

ABBY

Bonjour!

HERMIONE

(grumpily)

It's *bonsoir* if it's the evening.

ABBY

Oops, sorry! *Bonsoir* from our ski trip. We're really missing our Jess . . . who can't be with us at the moment – we won't go into why – BUT we are still having sooo much fun!

LUCY

I'm l-loving the skiing, but there's someone special missing . . . apart from Jessie . . . and I r-really wish he could be here too, especially as tomorrow is V-Valentine's Day.

Hi, S-Sam, if you're watching.

ABBY

Cute! And you're not the only one feeling the love!

ABBY nudges HERMIONE, who flinches.

ABBY (CONTINUED)

L'amour toujours! That means 'love forever', I think, and—

HERMIONE

(interrupting)

So I've researched some interesting facts about Valentine's Day and put together a little quiz. First question: what is the origin of Valentine's Day?

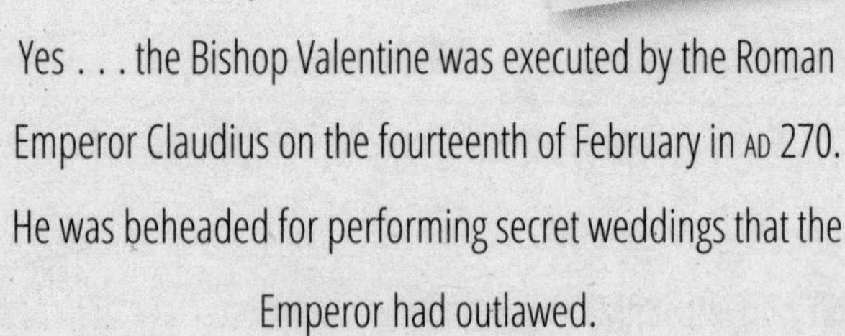

LUCY

Wasn't Valentine a s-saint or something?

HERMIONE

(bleakly)

Yes . . . the Bishop Valentine was executed by the Roman Emperor Claudius on the fourteenth of February in AD 270. He was beheaded for performing secret weddings that the Emperor had outlawed.

ABBY

(rolling her eyes)

Well, that's depressing! Isn't there something more cheerful?

HERMIONE

Not everything about love is good, you know. Fine. Who gave the first Valentine's card?

ABBY

Oh, no, Hermione, not another history question!

HERMIONE

(looking a bit annoyed)

OK, well how about this one? Why do we give chocolates on Valentine's Day?

LUCY

Isn't it s-something to do with the chemicals in chocolate? They make you happy?

ABBY

I don't need a quiz to tell me that! It's obvious!

HERMIONE

Yeah. Chocolate contains the same chemical our brain releases when we fall in love.

ABBY

(giggling)

Well, there's a lot of that chemical flowing around here tonight, right, girls? You too, Hermione.

HERMIONE whacks her arm.

ABBY (CONTINUED)

Ouch! So, now it's my turn to ask the questions . . . Do you believe in love at first sight? Lucy?

LUCY

I g-guess so! I mean, when I first saw my b-boyfriend, I had a funny feeling in my s-stomach . . . I felt almost sick.

HERMIONE

Are you sure that wasn't the smell of horse manure?

You were on a farm, remember!

LUCY

NO! It wasn't and I still get b-butterflies in my tummy when I think about him . . .

ABBY

Aw, that's so cute! Hope you're watching this, Sam!

What about you, H?

HERMIONE

(muttering)

Well . . . I guess you can tell when someone is special. Sadly, it doesn't always mean that the feeling is mutual, even if you really want it to be.

HERMIONE stares into space and LUCY gives her a concerned look.

ABBY

Well, I definitely believe in love at first sight; it just happens to me all the time! There are so many boys around that I can't keep up! Actually I have a Valentine's surprise for you, Lucy, from Sam.

ABBY passes a wrapped gift to LUCY, which she has been hiding under a cushion.

ABBY (CONTINUED)

Before we went away, he asked me to give it to you and this seems like a good time.

LUCY

No way! That is so th-thoughtful. I'll open it t-tomorrow.

ABBY

What? No! We're all dying to know what it is.
I'm the one who had to carry it the
whole way in my luggage!

LUCY

(a bit reluctantly)

OK . . . H,

do you know what this is?

HERMIONE

(shrugging)

No idea.

LUCY opens it slowly, and a smile creeps over her face. ABBY and HERMIONE look on eagerly.

LUCY

(embarrassed but pleased)

This is the c-cutest!

LUCY shows the camera a picture frame with a photo of SAM cuddling FOGHORN, her cat – with WE MISS YOU, LUCY! written across the front.

LUCY (CONTINUED)

Th-thank you, Sam, if you're watching.

HERMIONE

That is amazingly thoughtful. You've got a good one.

ABBY

Aw! I thought it was jewellery!

There is a knock at the door. ABBY gets up to open it.

BEN

Hey, we've been looking all over for you. As it's our last night, we thought we could have a bit of a part-ay!

ERIC

(walking into shot)

We found a pizza-delivery company and we've got some music . . . oops! Didn't realize you were filming.

ABBY

We're wrapping it up here anyway. Have a Love Heart!

ABBY hands BEN a sweet and he blushes.

HERMIONE

So it's goodbye from the mountains. Give us a thumbs-up if you liked our Girls Can Vlog on Tour videos.

LUCY

Even better – subscribe! And H-Happy Valentine's Day!

All three girls wave.

ABBY, HERMIONE and LUCY

Bye!

FADE OUT.

Views: 3,012

Subscribers: 7,478

Comments:

ShyGirl1: Wish I'd got a valentine. ☹

StalkerGurl: I got three! ❤❤❤

PuppyLove: Your boyfriend is so sweet, Lucy!

MagicMorgan: Party! Party!

queen_dakota: Ben. Call me.

PrankingsteinCharlie: You guys don't seem to be doing much skiing.

Amazing_Abby_xxx: Sorrrrry, Charlie! Excuse us for having fun!

girlscanvlogfan: This GCV Tour vlog is a big success! Really boosting your subs.

Sam: Missing my girl . . .

Adder1: Hey, Hermione, my gift to you is a fortune cookie. Hope it doesn't choke you!

MagicMorgan: I see the Slytherin snake has changed its name – please do us all a favour and slither off, once and for all.

(scroll down to see 77 more comments)

Chapter Nine

The Year 9s gathered in the hotel reception, a tired and sunburnt but happy group. Mostly happy.

'I can't w-wait to get home and see Sam,' said Lucy. 'It feels like we've been apart for ages!'

Hermione tried to smile but failed. She was still reeling from that fortune cookie comment, and for once she didn't feel like hearing about Lucy's perfect relationship. She was also dreading going home and having to face the truth about divorce-gate. The only consolation was that her grandmother Paw Paw would be there, and she was always warm and caring.

'Are you ok, H?' said Lucy carefully. 'Are you still

w-worried about seeing your p-parents, or is it something else?' Hermione had confided in Lucy after the odd message from her mum, and Lucy had encouraged her to talk to both her parents when she get home. *Easy for her to say,* Hermione thought now, uncharitably. *On top of having the world's sweetest boyfriend, her parents are happily married.* She knew she was being really unfair, and that her best friend was only trying to help, but she was in too terrible a mood to care.

'I'm fine,' she said.

'You sure?' Lucy checked. 'You didn't seem yourself when we were f-filming last night, either.'

'Look, just because I don't want to chat all the time doesn't mean there's anything wrong, OK?' she snapped. 'I like a bit of peace and quiet occasionally, so sue me.'

Lucy's eyes widened in surprise. 'Wow. Message received. G-guess I'll leave you alone then.' She walked briskly off to join Abby, who was busy trying to knock Ben's hat off his head.

Hermione welled up with tears. 'I'll help Hermione on

the coach first,' Miss Piercy told the group, just in time. 'Everyone else, stay here and check you've got all of your belongings. Mr Byrne, could you bring Hermione's bag please?'

Well, this is embarrassing, thought Hermione as she watched Mr Byrne dragging her suitcase along behind them.

'Hi there, Paul!' Miss Piercy greeted the bus driver. 'Good week?'

'Not bad.' He got out of the coach and stretched. 'I see we've got a casualty,' he remarked. 'You been in the wars, love?' he nodded at Hermione.

'It's just a sprain,' she said. *I can't wait for this stupid ankle to heal and for people to stop asking me stupid questions*, she thought.

Miss Piercy guided her into a seat near the front where she could rest her leg across the aisle. 'You get yourself comfortable, and Mr Byrne and I will round up the others. See you in a minute.'

'Thanks, miss,' she said. She took out her book while

she waited for everyone to join her on the coach.

'So relieved we don't have to deal with Puke-ota again,' said Eric as they all piled on a few minutes later. 'Not to mention Kayleigh and her epic smelly-food hauls.'

'Yes, I think we're all relieved about that. Hey, shove over, we're sitting there,' said Abby, making sure that she and Lucy got the seats nearest Hermione. Lucy gave Hermione a questioning glance.

'Sorry,' Hermione mouthed. But Lucy turned away again.

Hermione slumped down in her seat. For the thousandth time, she looked at the final text from Thierry, asking if they could be friends, then deleted it. Then, after a second, she deleted his number. There. Now she was completely friendless.

Well done, Hermione.

She didn't feel like vlogging and pretended to sleep for most of the journey home.

*

They arrived back at the school car park in the late evening. Hermione's dad had texted to say that he would be picking her up. She waited for everyone else to get off the coach, then hobbled off with Abby's help.

'Hi, Dad!' she called as he walked up to the coach. He hugged her then stood back, inspecting her anxiously.

'My poor little wounded soldier returning home from battle, huh?' he said. 'I hope you're not in too much pain?' He collected her suitcase from the pile on the pavement.

'Please, Dad, no more war jokes,' she said with a groan. 'I feel fine.' She hugged Abby goodbye, then hugged Lucy awkwardly too. She'd have to call her later to explain her rudeness.

Inside the car, her father moved the front seat back so that she had more room for her leg. 'So how come you're picking me up?' she asked. 'Where's Mum?'

'Your mum is at home, so don't worry. I'll take you over there now. And Paw Paw has arrived too so I'm sure she'll be spoiling you with her cooking,' he said, taking her hand and smiling at her. 'I just wanted to make sure

I caught a glimpse of you. I'm off on business next week, and I've missed you.'

'Oh,' she said, feeling pleased but slightly embarrassed. 'I missed you too.' It was actually really nice to see him and she didn't want to ruin the moment by asking awkward questions about the divorce. Maybe later.

As they set off, she opened the glove box to look for sweets. Rummaging around, she found a turquoise, silver-edged piece of material with pretty fringing. 'What's this?' she asked, pulling it out. 'A scarf?'

'Hmm?' asked Mr Chan, his eyes on the road. He glanced over quickly. 'Oh, that.'

'Not your colour, Dad,' she giggled, laying it out on her lap. 'I like it, though! Hang on, is this one of my birthday presents? You could at least have wrapped it. Where did you . . .' She trailed off, realizing that the atmosphere in the car had changed. Her dad was staring out at the road as if his life depended on it.

'Dad?' she asked urgently. 'What's wrong? Who does this belong to?'

'Doesn't matter.' He cleared his throat and there was silence for a few moments. 'So, how long do you have to keep the bandage on?' he said eventually.

'The doctor said – Wait, why are you changing the subject?' A dreadful feeling came over Hermione as she recalled some of her mother's comments. 'Dad. *Whose scarf is this?*'

He sighed loudly. 'OK. I was hoping we wouldn't have to have this conversation for a while, but . . . let me pull over here so we can talk.'

Hermione's mouth went dry. They were only a few streets away from home, but Mr Chan parked the car, then turned to face her. He tugged at the scarf.

'This scarf – this scarf belongs to one of my colleagues. Amy.'

'OK, so why is it in the car?' asked Hermione, her heart thudding.

'Hermione . . . ' Her father took her hand. 'You know your mother and I were happily married for many years. But unfortunately the situation has changed now, as

you already know. And, I have to tell you . . . Amy has something to do with that.'

Hermione snatched her hand away. 'What do you mean?' she asked fiercely. She knew what he was hinting at, but she couldn't believe it was true. Her mother's tired, sad face flashed through her mind.

Mr Chan sighed. 'Well. Over the last year or so your mother and I have grown apart.' Hermione winced. 'And since that happened, well, over time . . . I've fallen in love with someone else.'

'Amy?' gasped Hermione.

'Indeed. But you must understand, Hermione, things were already very difficult between me and your mother.' Hermione looked away, out of the window, as her father started talking at a million miles per hour. 'We tried to make it work, but it was only when I got to know Amy that I realized that was never going to happen. We'd had our time, we had YOU, we're still very proud of that, but now – a new chapter is beginning for us both.'

'Because you had an affair,' snapped Hermione.

'Well—'

'This whole thing is disgusting. Take me home – NOW.'

She burst into hot angry tears, refusing to accept a tissue and wiping her eyes on her coat sleeve. They drove off in silence, Hermione longing to a) see her mum and b) lock herself in her room forever.

Dear Diary,

We have a new contender for 'worst day of Hermione's life' – yesterday, I found out that my dad – my nice, sweet, dependable dad – IS HAVING AN AFFAIR. Yes, he cheated on Mum, with someone named AMY from WORK who he is STILL SEEING, and THAT IS THE REASON FOR THE DIVORCE!

And this whole time I've been blaming Mum and assuming she was the one who drove Dad away. No wonder she's been in a terrible mood!

I found hashtag AMY's scarf in Dad's car when he picked me up and he had to pull over and explain everything to me. It was a pretty dramatic scene. I cried and then refused to speak to him the whole way home. I could tell he was gutted, but why should I make him feel OK about his terrible life choices?

At least things have been better with Mum. When I got back, I told her immediately that I knew and she told me not to worry about her too much. She says she's had a while to adjust to what happened and that she's coping . . . But I'm still FUMING. How could Dad do that to our family? And I don't know why they didn't tell me the whole disgusting truth from the beginning. I'm not a child!

Paw Paw is calling me now, so I'd better go. Maybe she will help calm me down!!!

Hermione x

09:15

Unknown number: You haven't replied. I'm worried I hurt your feelings. I wanted to be clear, it's nothing personal. Things with me are kind of complicated right now. I'm single and I like you, but I'm not sure if I'm looking for a girlfriend, or ever will be . . . I'm still working things out, but in the meantime I really hope we can be friends. You're an amazing person. Tx

Update, Diary!

I got a message from Thierry. He was really sweet, and I think he was trying to tell me that he isn't necessarily . . . a hundred per cent into girls? I'm not sure, though. I do feel a bit better. What a day. Tomorrow I'm going to stay in bed and read and immerse myself in a fantasy world. Real life is too crazy!

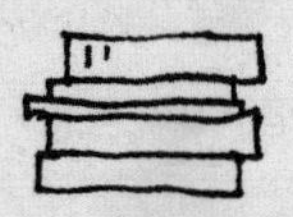

VLOG 9

online

Teaching My Grandma
Internet Slang

5:45

FADE IN: HERMIONE and her grandmother sitting next to each other on a sofa in HERMIONE's living room.

HERMIONE

Hi, guys! So today I'm going to do a vlog with my wonderful grandma. I call her Paw Paw cos that's the Chinese name for your mother's mother where my family comes from . . . so say hello, Paw Paw . . . and wave at the camera.

PAW PAW

(small wave)

Hello! Is that OK, Hermione?

HERMIONE

Brilliant! *(looks to camera)* Paw Paw's been asking me to show her what all this Girls Can Vlog stuff is about and I thought it would be fun to do a vlog together. So, Paw Paw, today I'm going to quiz you on some real-life and internet slang. Are you ready?

PAW PAW

(giggles)

As ready as I'll ever be! I hope this isn't going to be too embarrassing for you.

HERMIONE

Of course not! Let's get started. Paw Paw, what does 'totes' mean?

PAW PAW

'Totes'? You mean like a tote bag maybe? Something you carry around?

HERMIONE

(laughing)

Not quite. It means 'totally'. OK next one . . . what does 'bae' mean?

PAW PAW

'Bae'? Oh, I think I've heard that one . . . is it baby or babe?

HERMIONE

Close! It means the same sort of thing but it actually means 'before anyone else'.

PAW PAW

You mean a special person? Well, then you are my 'bae'!

HERMIONE

Ha ha . . . I love you for saying that. Usually it means your girlfriend or boyfriend, but who cares!

HERMIONE gives PAW PAW a quick hug.

HERMIONE (CONTINUED)

(still laughing)

Right, back to business!

Paw Paw, what does 'LOL' mean?

PAW PAW

Oh, I know this: lots of love!

HERMIONE

Well, sometimes . . . but there's another more common meaning?

I told you about it yesterday?

PAW PAW

Oh yes, lots of laughs!

HERMIONE

Close enough! It's 'laugh out loud'.

OK, what does 'slay' mean?

PAW PAW

'Slay'? I assume it's not like a one-horse open sleigh . . .

HERMIONE shakes her head no.

PAW PAW (CONTINUED)

'Slay' . . . hmmm . . . it might mean kill?

To slay a dragon?

HERMIONE

Not really, although I think it might come from that . . . 'Slay' is something you say when somebody's done something really good or impressive.

PAW PAW

Why not say congratulations, then?

HERMIONE

(laughing)

Good question! Well, you might . . . but 'slay' is a bit cooler.

How about 'on fleek'?

PAW PAW

'On fleek'? That doesn't sound very nice . . .

a bit like fleas?

HERMIONE

No, it's a compliment! I could say your outfit is 'on fleek'.

What would that mean?

PAW PAW

Oh, like trendy or in fashion?

So could we say that your haircut is 'on fleek'?

HERMIONE instantly puts her hands on her head to try to cover up her hair.

HERMIONE

(shrieking)

So NOT on fleek! But, yeah, basically. It means 'on point' or perfect. It's usually about eyebrows or make-up or something like that.

PAW PAW

(stroking Hermione's hair)

It will grow and be even more beautiful – you'll see! You need to put that oil I gave you on it every day.

HERMIONE

Yeah, morning and evening, right?

Sorry, guys!

Minor diversion! OK, Paw Paw, last question . . .

What does 'ship' mean?

PAW PAW

'Ship'? I suppose you don't mean anything like a boat . . . or sending something in the post?

HERMIONE

Nooo. Let me give you an example from Harry Potter . . . I really 'ship' Hermione and Harry. It means I really want them to be a couple. Unfortunately, that never happened . . .

PAW PAW

Oh well, it's only a book! This has been lovely, but now I need to get into the kitchen and start making the dim sum I promised you.

HERMIONE

Well, I wouldn't want to stop you doing that! It's my favourite . . . So thank you, Paw Paw, for taking part in my vlog. What do you need to say?

PAW PAW

(to camera)

If you liked this video, give us a thumbs-up. And subscribe to the Girls Can Vlog channel!

HERMIONE

Perfect! Love you, Paw Paw! Bye . . .

HERMIONE and PAW PAW blow kisses to the camera – then burst out laughing.

FADE OUT.

Views: 3,249

Subscribers: 7,612

Comments:

RedVelvet: LOVE your grandma!

lucylocket: So cute! Paw Paw is awesome.

MagicMorgan: Grandma on fleek!

Amazing_Abby_xxx: Slay!

peterpranks: Hilarious! Might try this with my gran.

SassySays: This was hashtag *adorable*

Anaconda: Why don't u and ur grandma learn the slang for GO BACK TO YOUR OWN COUNTRY?

(scroll down to see 60 more comments)

Chapter Ten

On Sunday morning Hermione was downstairs at her laptop, hanging out on Mugglenet. She was immersed in a quiz called 'Can you name the characters treated by Poppy Pomfrey in the seven books of the Harry Potter series?' when her grandmother walked into the room, wrapping her beautiful silk dressing gown around her.

'Can I watch the video again, Hermione?' she asked. 'Or should I say "bae".'

'Of course, bae,' said Hermione with a smile. It was cute how much Paw Paw loved seeing herself onscreen. 'Come and sit next to me.'

She clicked on the Girls Can Vlog bookmark and brought up the video.

Yay! It's getting loads of views, she thought. As the music started to play, she noticed a few new comments below. 'Why don't u and ur grandma learn the slang for GO BACK TO YOUR OWN COUNTRY' said one of them. She froze. Then another comment, by the same user: 'Extra fried rice, make it snappy.' Feeling sick, Hermione hastily scrolled back up so that her grandmother couldn't read them. The thought of Paw Paw being hurt by these racist remarks was too awful to think about.

Once Paw Paw had watched the video again – 'We look very nice, don't we?' she said proudly – and had gone upstairs to have her bath, Hermione stared at the comments. For a few moments she just sat there, breathing deeply and trying not to panic. Next, she WhatsApped her friends and called an emergency meeting. She asked Abby if they could do it at her house because she didn't want her mum or grandmother overhearing their discussion. They arranged to meet that afternoon. Hermione still felt kind of awkward about seeing Lucy after their spat, but this issue had to be dealt with.

Josh opened the door. 'Hey, Hermione! Welcome back!' He glanced down at her crutches. 'Whoa, how's the ankle?'

'Not too bad, thanks,' she replied, hopping over the step into the hallway. Her mum had dropped her off at the door. 'Just a sprain, though it put an end to my Olympic skiing dreams!'

He laughed. 'Such a tragedy for the sport! Oh well, me and Charlie watched all your vlogs – it looked like you guys had an amazing time despite everything.' He closed the door and Weenie ran up to him. 'Wait! I'm trying to train him to walk on his hind legs so that we can film him later. We're thinking of launching a Prankingstein spin-off channel, PrankingPug! What do you reckon?'

'Cool idea!' Hermione grinned. 'I'd definitely subscribe.' She heard voices coming from upstairs.

'Sounds like they're ready for me. I might leave my crutches here – I can manage without them.' She propped them up at the bottom of the stairs then walked slowly up.

'Yay, you made it!' she cried when she saw Jessie a few moments later. She and Abby were hunched over Abby's computer. 'I thought you were grounded – like forever?'

'Yeah, but I told my mum what was going on with this trolling and she agreed I could come to this meeting, because it's so important,' said Jessie, standing up and giving Hermione a hug. 'Plus I think she's starting to believe me about being set up by the despicable duo.'

'That's good,' said Hermione, just as Lucy arrived. 'I still can't believe you actually got sent home.'

'It was the worst day of my life,' said Jessie. 'That journey home was so bad – I definitely sense trouble in Bakota Land. Dakota was moaning the whole trip, when she wasn't puking that is. Anyway, I'm still annoyed about missing out on the rest of the week – I just feel like such a fool!'

'Oh, Jess, you're not a fool, but maybe just too trusting in people's good natures!' said Hermione sympathetically.

'Maybe,' said Jess. 'Hey, Luce.'

'Hi.' Lucy looked upset. 'I'm s-so angry about all of the comments, Hermione,' she said, throwing her coat on the bed. 'What is wrong with people?'

'I'm still reading through them,' said Abby from the computer. Hermione had decided not to delete them before the others had a chance to read them, but she hated the fact that they'd been out there for ages, for anyone to see.

'Come over and look,' continued Abby. 'Loads of our viewers are sticking up for you, H, and calling this person out.'

Hermione sighed, sitting down on the bed. She didn't feel like looking at the comments again. 'That's really sweet of them, but I've gotta say I'm getting massively creeped out. I've blocked this person three times and every time they come back with a different user name.'

'Yep. They're d-definitely persistent,' said Lucy. 'It makes you w-wonder if they have a life, other than t-trolling people online.'

Hermione nodded. 'I know, right? And it's weird that the comments have been directed at me specifically. I've been trying to ignore them, but it's really getting to me.' She took a breath. 'I mean, I know Dakota gives us all grief, but this is on another level – and really personal. I haven't heard nasty comments about my ethnicity in a long time.' Hermione could feel herself getting choked up. 'It's just so uncool.'

Abby and Jessie nodded sympathetically. 'I saw they d-dragged your grandmother into it too,' added Lucy, putting her arm round Hermione. 'What a nasty p-piece of work they must be.'

'I just don't get what they have against me,' said Hermione. 'I don't have any enemies . . . that I know of. Do they just hate me because I'm Chinese? Why would they? And why do they even watch our channel if they hate me so much?'

There was an awkward silence. None of them had an answer for her. Abby minimized the tab so that they wouldn't have to look at the comments. Hermione sat there unhappily for a few moments, then decided it was time to tell them about her decision.

'Anyway, guys,' she mumbled, picking at her bandage. She took a deep breath. 'This is really hard for me, but . . . I've decided to quit the channel.'

'What!' cried Abby. 'But you can't!' She looked at Lucy and Jessie. 'Guys, tell her!'

Hermione stiffened. She'd known this wouldn't go down well, but now that the moment had come she realized it was going to be much harder to explain than she'd thought. The channel was a truly important part of their friendship.

'Abby's right!' said Jessie frantically. 'You can't let that idiot get to you, Hermione – that means they've won.'

There was another uncomfortable silence.

This is horrible, thought Hermione.

'I think we should all chill out a bit,' said Lucy anxiously.

'H has obviously had a really t-traumatic time and we should listen to w-what she has to say.' Hermione felt a surge of love and gratitude for her best friend. 'If you want to tell us, that is?'

'I do,' said Hermione, her voice wavering. 'Sorry to sound so pathetic, but basically I've had the worst week of my life. You know about Thierry, obviously, but there's also been some stuff about my parents and their divorce that I don't really want to talk about.' She paused, afraid she would start crying. She saw Abby look questioningly at Lucy, and Lucy shrugged. She hadn't told either of them about the Amy thing.

'Here,' said Jessie, getting up suddenly and grabbing a box of chocolate truffles from the bookshelf. She dumped them on to Hermione's lap. 'You need these. Now.'

'Hey! I got those in France!' cried Abby. 'They weren't cheap you know!' Hermione giggled despite herself as Abby came to her senses. 'I mean, yes, please help yourself. Have loads.'

'Thanks, Abs.' Hermione passed them round and unwrapped one, popping it in her mouth. The creamy sweetness made her feel better almost instantly and she felt ready to open up to her friends. 'So yeah. It's like, sprained ankle, rejected by a boy, horrid family stuff . . . I just can't deal with poisonous comments from creepy trolls on top of that.' She swallowed the chocolate and picked up another one. 'All I want to do is bury myself in books and escape my crazy life.' She waved the chocolate around in the air. 'And stuff my face with chocolate! I just don't feel like being funny and cute on camera right now.'

Lucy nodded. 'I t-totally get it. Sometimes things just overwhelm you – we've all b-been there.'

Hermione saw that Abby was going pink with the effort of not saying anything. 'I know it's rubbish for the channel, Abs,' she added with a sigh. 'You guys can carry on without me, though, you're all amazing!'

Abby looked at her uncertainly. 'But our viewers always say the best videos are the ones with all four of us.'

'Yeah, but they'll get used to it,' said Hermione. 'So there will be a bit less content about books and baking – that doesn't matter.' She pointed as Jessie got off the bed and did the splits. 'Look, amazing video content right here!' But her attempt at humour fell on deaf ears.

Suddenly Jessie responded. 'Obviously we can't force you to stay, Hermione, but you wanna know what I think?'

Hermione sighed. 'Do I?'

Jessie wriggled out of the splits and sat down on the floor, twisting herself into the lotus position. 'I think making videos helps us take our minds off the difficult stuff, like your parents' divorce, or Abby's problems with schoolwork, or Lucy's stutter. Like, we've all got a lot going on, and for ninety-nine per cent of the time this channel is a really fun distraction! And I don't think you should forget that because of one mean person.'

'She has a p-point,' said Lucy softly. 'Don't you think, H?'

'I do understand, H,' Jessie continued, 'because I've

suffered from nasty racist abuse too occasionally and, just because I'm a bit of a joker and laugh it off, it doesn't mean it doesn't hurt.'

Hermione's thoughts were a blur. She knew what Jessie was saying made sense, but she'd also promised herself to be firm and stick to her decision. It was her life, after all. She would miss vlogging, though.

'Besides,' said Abby, who was now brushing her hair energetically. 'Think of our subscriber count. We can't lose our following, we just can't.' Hermione stiffened. *Was that all Abby cared about?* She rolled her eyes at Jessie, but Abby didn't notice and kept on talking. 'We need to keep creating excellent content to keep growing our subscribers; if one of us leaves, our numbers will plummet. We're doing so well right now, and we need to keep aiming for that twenty-thousand target.'

'Abs,' said Jessie firmly. 'Can we have less of your business brain right now? In case you'd forgotten, Hermione has been on the receiving end of some racist abuse.' She looked at Hermione in concern. 'She doesn't

understand what it's like. The important thing is how you feel. We just want what's best for you.'

'Oh, r-right, of course,' stammered Abby, her eyes wide. 'Sorry, H, I didn't think.'

But Hermione's feelings, already raw enough, had been hurt one time too many. She got off the bed and hobbled over to the door, resting against its frame. 'I've made up my mind. I'm sure Girls Can Vlog will do amazingly without me and the numbers won't suffer. I bet nobody will even realize I've gone.'

'H . . .' started Lucy. They all stared at her in dismay.

'I have to go now,' said Hermione, her heart racing. She hated all this drama and attention. 'I just need some time on my own. I'll see you guys at school.' She waved half-heartedly, left the room and promptly dissolved into tears.

VLOG 10

FADE IN: LUCY, JESSIE and ABBY sitting on ABBY's bed, looking serious.

ABBY

So this is going to be a short but very important video. It's about the problem of internet trolling and what to do about it.

JESSIE

The word 'trolling' makes it sound like it's maybe something cute and not that serious . . . so actually we should call it cyberbullying, which is what it really is.

LUCY

I th-think it's really s-sad that people want to be so mean. Any kind of b-bullying is unacceptable.

ABBY

The thing is we all know that when you decide to vlog you are putting yourself out there. You're asking for comments and reactions and you don't really expect everyone to like you or what you are doing.

JESSIE

True, but there's a big difference between that and the really vicious, personal comments some people make. And racist remarks are totally off limits.

LUCY

(nodding)

I think s-some people think they can say anything onscreen and that somehow it's n-not real. They say things they wouldn't d-dare say to your face.

JESSIE

Yeah, my mum says it's probably because they feel bad about themselves and they want to pull others down, but, whatever the reason, spreading hatred around the internet is never cool. It makes me feel so angry and frustrated that people feel like it's OK to do that.

ABBY

So what can you do if you get abusive comments on YouTube?

Firstly you can remove the offensive comments, block the sender and report them using the reporting tool page, and YouTube will investigate.

It might be a good idea to take a screenshot of any comment as evidence.

LUCY

The t-trouble is – as we've discovered – that trolls may be p-persistent and reappear under another name.

JESSIE

I think the answer is to ignore them. If you answer back, you just encourage them. If you don't, they will eventually give up. Just don't interact!

LUCY

It's h-hard, though, especially when it's very h-hurtful, but remember what the b-bunny in *Bambi* said: 'If you can't say something nice, don't say nothing at all.'

JESSIE, LUCY and ABBY laugh.

JESSIE

It's true! So if you're the victim of any cyberbullying, be sure to report it. Also, tell your friends and family so they can support you. If it's happening at school, tell your teachers. Don't suffer in silence! Stay strong!

ABBY

Don't get us wrong – we love YouTube – but it's important to keep it a safe and positive place. We hope this video was helpful to any of you out there that are having problems with bullying for any reason. Feel free to share your experiences in the comments below. See you soon! Bye!

They all wave.

FADE OUT.

Views: 3,416

Subscribers: 7,945

Comments:

RedVelvet(verified)**:** This is brilliant, guys! Stay strong!

PrankingsteinCharlie: Be Your Own Hero!

Gamegirl2000: Very inspiring. Gave me goosebumps x

girlscanvlogfan: So proud of you!

ShyGirl1: People bully me calling me skinny. It's so upsetting.

Anonymousgirl: I've been getting so much hate on my own channel. I was gonna quit but now I've changed my mind. Thanks. Xxx

MagicMorgan: Yeah! Don't give in to these idiots.

xoxoCamilla: That was such a great video and makes me realize I'm not alone.

(scroll down to see 89 more comments)

Chapter Eleven

From: TheRealRedVelvet100@gmail.com

To: HashtagHermione@hermionesworld.com

Hi, Hermione!

I know this is a bit out of the blue, but I thought this might be a good time to get in touch. So, Abby filled me in about the horrible trolling you guys, and particularly you, have experienced recently. Firstly, I wanted to say how sorry I am to hear that – every YouTuber has had experience of nasty comments – and I wanted to let you know that you're not alone. People have commented on me being mixed race, on whether I've gained weight, on what I'm wearing, all kinds of things.

Ultimately I had to choose whether to let this negative energy get me down or not. Whether it would stop me doing this thing I love. And in the end I decided to let it go. Of course, I still have my bad days where those comments can really drag me down, but I do my best to focus on the lovely positive things that most of my viewers say to me, and I feel better for it.

Anyway, I wanted to say I'm here for you, if you ever want to talk. I've loved watching your channel grow and you guys have gone from strength to strength, but I know it's not as easy as it looks, so I'm here to help you take the rough with the smooth.

Good luck!

Tiffany x

Hermione stared at the screen on her laptop. Even though Girls Can Vlog had made a couple of videos

with the super-famous Tiffany (or RedVelvet as she was better known), she still thought of her as Abby's friend more than hers, so it was an amazing surprise to receive such a personal email from her. And she was touched by Tiffany's words. It had never occurred to her that someone as successful and talented as RedVelvet would receive online abuse too.

Hermione was still feeling confused. She'd come home after an awkward day at school of trying to act normal around the others, but avoiding conversations about her decision to quit. Her dad had been calling and messaging her too, but she still didn't feel ready to talk to him.

'Are you busy with homework, Hermione?' asked Paw Paw, tapping at her open door.

'Not really,' said Hermione, snapping out of her daze. 'Just reading an email. Come in!'

Paw Paw came and stood over her, kissing the top of her head. 'Your mother has gone to the supermarket so I thought I would come and chat with my favourite granddaughter.'

'Your only granddaughter,' said Hermione cheekily.

Her grandmother chuckled. '*And* my favourite! So, who is this email from? Anyone interesting?'

Hermione considered lying and closing the screen, but then something came over her. She was tired of keeping all the horrible secrets to herself and she wanted to tell her grandmother everything, even at the risk of upsetting her. Mum would definitely overreact if she told her, but maybe Paw Paw would understand. Ever since Hermione was little, she had a knack of knowing how to make her feel better.

'It's from a famous YouTuber – RedVelvet. She filmed with us a couple of times,' explained Hermione. 'She's got millions of subscribers and it was a real honour.'

'That sounds exciting,' said Paw Paw with a smile, pulling up a chair. 'And she emails you?'

Hermione cleared her throat and turned to look at her grandmother. 'Well, actually this is the first time she's emailed me. I had a problem – and she's giving me some advice.'

'What problem?' Paw Paw's eyes went back to the screen, skimming the lines of text. 'Horrible trolling? What does that mean, "trolling"? You didn't teach me that during our slang lesson. Hmm?'

Hermione grinned ruefully. 'No. It means . . . kind of bullying someone online. By leaving mean comments.'

Her grandmother looked at her anxiously. 'This I have heard of. But why would anyone attack you? What has been said?'

'I'm . . . I don't know, Paw Paw,' said Hermione. 'They made nasty comments linked to me being Chinese. That's racist, right? I don't know who they are, but I've got so upset about it that I've decided to quit YouTube. It's for the best.'

'Poor girl,' said her grandmother, stroking the side of Hermione's face. 'This must have been so tough on you and I'm very angry on your behalf.' Then her eyes lit up with steely determination. 'But, you know what, this is a good lesson for you.'

'Really?' said Hermione in surprise. 'I feel like it's a

lesson I could happily have lived without! Paw Paw, they said mean things about our family!'

Her grandmother frowned. 'What exactly did they say?' Then she said, 'Wait, don't tell me. I don't need to hear it! The best thing to do with hate speech is to stifle it. Don't repeat it; don't listen to it.' She looked at Hermione. 'Making that video with you the other day, I was so proud of my little Hermione!'

Hermione grinned. 'Paw Paw! You're embarrassing me!'

'Not just how well you interviewed me and spoke on camera, like a confident young lady,' continued Paw Paw, 'but also how you prepared the camera, and the lights and sound – a true professional! You've only been doing this YouTube for a short time, but look how far you've come. It would be such a shame to stop now.'

'I guess . . .' said Hermione, glowing at her grandmother's words. It was the first time anyone in her family had shown real interest in her vlogging and all of a sudden she felt very proud of herself too.

I have *learned a lot. Like, loads!*

'You used to be so shy, always alone with your books, and now you are flourishing, like a flower unfurling its petals.'

Enough of the dodgy similes, thought Hermione, cringing. Imagine if her friends could hear this conversation!

Her grandmother stood up. 'That's enough from your Paw Paw. It's your choice, of course. As long as my Hermione is happy.' She checked her watch. 'I'm going to start on the dinner before your mum comes back and shouts at me for not chopping the vegetables.'

Hermione smiled and glanced back at her screen, just as a new email pinged up from an address she didn't recognize . . .

Dear Diary,

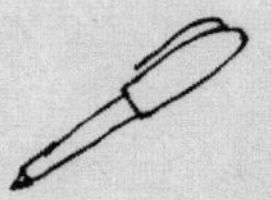

OMG! You will never guess what. I've been chosen as a finalist for the creative-writing competition I entered. They said

my entry was 'beautifully written, showing real flair and originality'. Aahhhhhhhh! Can it be true?! They said there were hundreds of entries so the odds were stacked against me.

I've just told Mum and Paw Paw over dinner and I was allowed a tiny glass of wine to celebrate. (It was gross.)

I might even call Dad even though I still HATE him.

This might be the best moment of my life, EVER.

It means I get to take part in a writers' workshop with the other finalists, which is part of YA Writing Con. OM actual G.

It's not for a few months so my ankle will have healed properly by then. Is it wrong that I want to vlog it, even though I've quit the channel? I'm so confused! But mainly happy – for the first time in ages!

Hermione x

VLOG 11

FADE IN: Daytime. ABBY's family room. ABBY, LUCY and JESSIE are sitting at a large table with JOSH and CHARLIE from the Prankingstein channel. The top of the table and the floor around them is covered in plastic sheeting.

ABBY

So today the Girls Can Vlog crew are going to have some collab fun with Prankingstein!

CHARLIE

You bet! We're gonna do the Eat It or Wear It Challenge . . .

ABBY

(gesturing at objects laid out on the table)

OK, so we have a load of delicious food, like whipped cream, baked beans and yoghurt – and some horrible stuff, like cider vinegar, sauerkraut and . . .

LUCY

Cat food! So we have two b-bowls filled with paper slips: One has the names of the foods or drinks and the other has the w-words 'eat' or 'wear'.

JOSH

One team picks the food and the other picks the 'eat' or 'wear' and then the first team has to either eat or wear it.

JESSIE

(laughing)

'Wear' it really means dump it on someone's head or smear it on their face!

ABBY

OK, let's get started.

JOSH burps loudly.

ABBY (CONTINUED)

(squeals)

Yuck, Josh, you're so disgusting!

JOSH

Just warming up! Ladies first . . .

ABBY reaches into the first bowl and picks a slip of paper.

ABBY

(grimaces)

Baked Beans. Eat it or . . . wear it?

CHARLIE

(gleefully)

Now I get to pick . . .

CHARLIE picks a folded piece of paper from the second bowl.

CHARLIE (CONTINUED)

Ha ha, bad luck! It's 'wear' it!

ABBY

Oh, no! I just washed my hair . . . Can't I just eat it?

Pretty please?

CHARLIE shakes his head, grins and then dumps the open tin of beans over ABBY's head. ABBY shrieks as cold beans drip down her face. LUCY covers her mouth with a hand to hide her laughter as she hands ABBY a towel.

CHARLIE

Bonus! You get to eat them as well!

ABBY

(wiping beans off her face)

Eeew!

ABBY shoves CHARLIE in mock anger.

ABBY (CONTINUED)

I can't believe you dumped the whole tin on me!

I HATE this game!

JOSH

My turn!

JOSH picks a slip of paper from the first bowl.

JOSH (CONTINUED)

Cider vinegar! Ugh. Could be bad . . .

LUCY picks a slip out of the second bowl.

LUCY

And it's 'eat' or I s-suppose 'drink' in this case.

LUCY pours some vinegar into a tablespoon and holds it up to JOSH's mouth.

JOSH

It smells like cat's pee! I can't drink that . . . I'll be sick . . .

LUCY

Don't be a ch-chicken!

JOSH holds his nose, opens his mouth and closes his eyes as

LUCY tips the contents of the spoon into his mouth. JOSH makes a choking noise and then runs to spit out the vinegar off-camera.

ABBY

That was cheating!

You're supposed to swallow it!

JESSIE

Your turn, Luce.

LUCY pulls a slip out of the first bowl and sighs.

LUCY

Hot chilli sauce.

JOSH grabs a slip from the second bowl.

JOSH

And it says 'eat'! OK, Lucy, let's see just how tough you are . . .

LUCY

OK, here g-goes!

LUCY takes a spoonful of chilli sauce, swallows it, grimaces – then her face relaxes.

LUCY (CONTINUED)

It's not that bad really . . . hang on . . . HELP!

My m-mouth is burning!

Water . . . I need water!

LUCY grabs a drink and downs it in one.

ABBY

Jess, you're up now . . .

JESSIE

Wish me luck!

JESSIE rifles through the first bowl – seemingly reluctant to choose.

CHARLIE

Come on, Jess, don't be a wimp!

JESSIE holds up a slip.

JESSIE

(staring in disbelief at the piece of paper in her hand)

OH NO! It's not fair . . .

I got the worst one.

It's cat food!

ABBY, LUCY, JOSH and CHARLIE holler with excitement.

JESSIE (CONTINUED)

Will I have to eat it or wear it? Charlie, my fate is in your hands!

CHARLIE pulls a slip out of the second bowl, opens it and raises his eyebrows.

CHARLIE

So sorry, Jess . . . it's 'eat'.

JESSIE

(smelling the spoonful of cat food)

Ugh. I don't know if I can do it . . . I'm gagging already . . .

JOSH

It's not *THAT* bad . . . I've eaten dog food before . . .

JESSIE

Wanna take my place?

JESSIE shoves the spoon in JOSH's face and he recoils.

JESSIE (CONTINUED)

No, didn't think so! Here goes nothing!

JESSIE takes a little bit of the cat food into her mouth, chews quickly and swallows. LUCY thrusts a drink into JESSIE's hand.

JESSIE (CONTINUED)

Actually, it wasn't that bad . . . NOT!

LUCY

Oh, I'm sooo s-sorry, Jess.

You were so brave.

CHARLIE

(giving Jessie an encouraging pat on the shoulder)

Jess, you are a trooper!

ABBY

So, Charlie, I think you're the last one remaining . . .

CHARLIE pulls out a slip of paper from the first bowl and smiles.

CHARLIE

It's my lucky day!

I got whipped cream.

I absolutely LOVE whipped cream . . .

ABBY

Ah, but what will you have to do with your whipped cream?

ABBY laughs flirtatiously as she reads the slip she has drawn from bowl.

ABBY (CONTINUED)

And the answer is . . . 'wear' it!

CHARLIE

Damn! I was hoping for a treat . . .

ABBY takes the spray can of whipped cream and walks over to CHARLIE.

ABBY

(smiling menacingly)

Where shall I start?

ABBY starts spraying the whipped cream all over CHARLIE's face while giggling. First she outlines his eyebrows and next she puts dots of cream on his cheeks and nose.

ABBY (CONTINUED)

You look so cute! Now, open up!

CHARLIE opens his mouth and ABBY fills it with whipped cream and starts smearing it on to his lips.

CHARLIE

(through a mouthful of cream)

Wanna try some, Abs? I'm happy to share?

ABBY and CHARLIE both giggle hysterically.

JOSH

(covering his eyes)

OK, guys, enough! This is gonna need an X-rating in a minute so let's call it quits.

JESSIE

(laughing)

If you enjoyed this video, smash the thumbs-up button and subscribe to our channels: Girls Can Vlog and Prankingstein, and, if you have any ideas for future collabs we could do, place them in the comments down below!

ALL

(waving manically)

Bye!

FADE OUT.

Views: 4,508

Subscribers: 8,713

Comments:

peterpranks: Cat food? LOL! How about the Try Not to Laugh Challenge?

StalkerGurl: Eyebrows on fleek, Charlie!

MagicMorgan: Chabby! ❤❤❤

So-Cal-Gal: Loving the whipped cream!

girlscanvlogfan: Nearly at 10,000 ☺

queen_dakota: The baked beans were an improvement . . .

RedVelvet(verified)**:** Great to see you all back!

(scroll down to see 73 more comments)

Chapter Twelve

The next weekend, Hermione sat in the kitchen catching up with her favourite YouTube channels. She knew the girls were having a meeting this morning before Lucy had to rush off to her city farm volunteer job. Abby had invited Hermione to come round later to hang out with her and Jessie afterwards. 'We promise not talk about the channel,' they'd said.

Hermione watched the latest videos on RedVelvet's vlogging channel before checking out the latest Girls Can Vlog video – a collab with Prankingstein. Soon she was giggling over her cereal. It was so funny – no wonder the views were so high.

Abby's clearly into Charlie again – no doubt about it.

And seeing the video confirmed what Hermione's heart had been telling her. She'd been mulling it over all week and now she knew for sure.

'Do you want to come with me and Paw Paw to this new gallery opening?' asked her mum, popping her head into the kitchen.

'No,' she said, 'but . . . could you drop me off at Abby's?' She suddenly couldn't wait to tell her friends about her decision . . . assuming they agreed with it, of course.

Abby's mum let her in half an hour later and she tiptoed up the stairs. She could hear Abby speaking loudly. 'Guys, you are not going to BELIEVE what I have to tell you,' she was saying. Hermione smiled fondly. Always such a drama queen.

'Sorry to interrupt,' she said nervously, coming into the room. Weenie jumped off the bed and ran round in circles, yapping at her. 'Hi Weenie!'

Abby looked confused. 'I thought you were coming

later? It's great to see you, but we're still in the middle of our meeting – is that OK?'

'Yeah,' said Hermione. 'Sorry to interrupt, but I have something to say to you guys.' She smiled at the floor, unable to look any of them in the eye. 'I actually want back in. If you'll have me, that is.'

Lucy and Jessie shrieked and ran over to hug her. 'Of course, we want you, lunatic!' said Jessie. Hermione glanced over her head at Abby, who was standing there looking at them, unsmiling.

'How about you, Abs?' she asked nervously. *Does Abby hate me now? Is it too late?*

Abby continued to stare at her for a few seconds before bursting into laughter and joining the group hug. 'KIDDING! I'M HASHTAG *THRILLED* YOU'RE BACK!' she cried. 'ESPECIALLY because of the news I'm about to share with you all.'

'What news?' asked Lucy.

'Yeah, haven't we had enough news recently?' said Jessie, rolling her eyes. 'I just want things to go

back to normal. Jeez. I'm exhausted!'

'This is GOOD news, Jess!' said Abby, climbing up and standing on the bed. She cleared her throat. 'So, I was FaceTiming Tiffany earlier. Turns out our scrumptious RedVelvet wants us to attend SummerTube with her.'

'What?' gasped Jess. 'As in, that massive YouTube convention in London they have every summer?'

Abby grinned. 'The very same. And this year the theme is "fresh talent" – people who only started up their YouTube channel in the past twelve months. All the famous YouTubers have been asked to nominate their favourite newbie to come along as their guests, and Tiffany chose us. We get to stay in a hotel and everything!'

The girls started jumping and screeching, and Abby continued, 'The reason Tiffany was calling was to check if we were all up for it.' She glanced at Hermione. 'So, you're definitely back in?'

'Are you k-kidding? After THAT news? Of course she is!' yelled Lucy.

Hermione grinned. 'Lucy's right. SummerTube sounds completely amazing. I wouldn't miss it for anything! But I wanted to come back anyway. I have such a great time with you guys and I'm so proud of our channel. I just needed a break.'

'Well said, H!' yelled Jessie, 'You're the best!'

Hermione giggled and kissed Weenie on the nose. 'It's not all roses – I still need to grow out my hair before I go anywhere near SummerTube.'

Later Hermione was in her room, feverishly jotting down vlog ideas. There was a knock at the front door, then another. Her mum and Paw Paw were still out, so she ran downstairs and opened it. She blinked. Her dad was standing on the doorstep with a very upset-looking girl by his side. She looked a couple of years younger than Hermione.

'Hermione,' Mr Chan said with a slight frown. 'Is your mother here?'

'No . . .' said Hermione, baffled. The girl

sniffed, looking down at her shoes.

'Never mind,' said her father. 'It's actually you we need to see. Felicity here has something to say to you. May we?'

He barged into the front room, the pale-faced girl trailing miserably behind him.

Hermione was too confused to remember to be angry with her father. Who was this girl and what could she possibly have to say to Hermione?

'Look. I'm sorry to introduce you two under such difficult circumstances, but Felicity is Amy's daughter,' explained her father, avoiding Hermione's eye. 'And, like you, she was extremely upset when she found out that her mother and I were seeing each other. Which is completely understandable. What is less understandable and completely unacceptable is how Felicity chose to express her anger about the situation. Felicity?'

A pause. 'I'm really sorry,' mumbled Felicity, glancing up at Hermione.

Brain overload . . . brain overload . . . thought Hermione, struggling to process that this 'Amy' had a daughter too. *And why is she apologizing to me? Sure, the situation is terrible, but it's not her fault!*

'What are you sorry for, Felicity?' prompted Mr Chan gently.

'For . . . for what I wrote. The nasty comments. I didn't mean it. I was just really upset.' The girl wiped a tear from her eye. 'I actually love your channel and I don't want you to quit.'

Hermione stared at her, then gasped. It couldn't be . . . surely?

Dear Diary,

Today is not the worst, but definitely the *weirdest* day of my life.

It turns out that my troll is a twelve-year-old girl! Felicity, who is Amy's daughter. Yes, THAT Amy. Her mum introduced her to Dad a few weeks ago and he told her about

Girls Can Vlog. He thought she would like the channel and it might be a way for us to become friends (ha ha, as if), but instead she decided to . . . well, bully me horrendously! She's really sorry about it now; her parents are splitting up too and she says she was so unhappy she didn't fully realize what she was doing.

It's so bizarre – I imagined the troll to be some creepy grown-up man. I'm relieved about that. Felicity says she went down the racist route because she thought it would be the most hurtful (newsflash: she was right!!), but she couldn't deal with the guilt . . . especially when she saw the video about trolling and realized I'd been so badly hurt, so she confessed everything to her mum, who told Dad. Weird, huh?

Mum was absolutely FURIOUS when she heard all this and really shouted at Dad. Drama all round. My dad wants me to meet up with Felicity again, though, and her mum, Amy, too, but that won't be happening any time soon! I'm still SO angry with Dad and I can't believe he thinks I would want to be friends with the daughter of the woman who he cheated on Mum with – AND who made me leave my

beloved Girls Can Vlog with her creepy comments!

Speaking of which, in other weird but this time WONDERFUL news, we found out earlier that we've been invited to SummerTube by RedVelvet. How amazing is that?! This brilliant news right after being chosen as a finalist in the writing competition has put me on top of the world. Maybe it's true that if you work through the difficult times you'll be rewarded eventually. I've also been chatting loads with Thierry online, which has been awesome. I've never really been friends with a guy before, and he's so funny. I think he'll call me 'Mademoiselle Harry Potter' forever!

Anyway, I'd better go – I've got GCV homework. We're working so hard at making our videos the best they can be before the convention, and I need to get brainstorming for new content. As Abby always says, our fans deserve nothing but the best.

Love you loads, Diary!

Hermione x

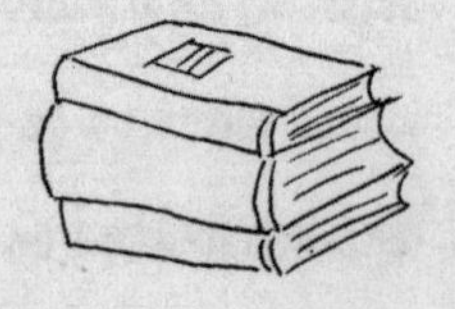

VLOG 12

FADE IN: HERMIONE sitting cross-legged on her bed, surrounded by books, pins and tote bags.

HERMIONE

Hello, guys! I'm back home after an amazing weekend at YA Writing Con. No exaggeration, it was THE BEST THING EVER. Here's a taste of what it was like . . .

EDITED MONTAGE: Hall full of teenagers, long queues, authors signing books and chatting to people, panels of speakers in front of an audience, people walking around in cosplay costumes . . .

TRANSITION: Back to HERMIONE's room

HERMIONE (CONTINUED)

So, I thought I was going to be able to vlog a lot more while I was there, but that didn't really happen. Sorry, guys! I found it hard juggling the camera with my tote bags full of swag and books. I queued for almost two hours to get a copy of *The Fault in Our Stars* signed by John Green. It is now my most treasured possession. Got a selfie with him too – check out my Instagram!

(she grins)

The main reason I was there was to take part in a teen writers' workshop on the Sunday. I'd entered a competition to win a place on it and I was one of the ten who made it – whoop! I may upload my entry on my blog . . . if I feel brave enough! The workshop leader made us introduce ourselves and read a little bit from our competition entries . . . Everyone's pieces were amazing and I felt really nervous. I could hardly open my mouth, but when I started speaking it was OK. Much scarier than vlogging, weirdly!

(she looks at her notes)

So, we did loads of writing exercises throughout the day, then also had to talk about our favourite author and favourite

character and explain why we liked them the most. I'm sure everyone can guess who I chose!

(laughs)

I also made special friends with this really cool girl who's fifteen. She's working on a sci-fi novel and has already written a hundred pages! I am sooo impressed! Anyway, we're going to stay in touch and maybe be NaNoWriMo buddies.

(looks at notebook again)

At the end of the workshop we got the opportunity to meet with a new author, Eve Pinewood, whose book has just come out and is already a bestseller. She'd studied on the same writing course as our workshop leader. I was really tongue-tied, but she was so cool and friendly that I loosened up and she told us all about what it's like to get your book published, how you work with editors, stuff like that . . .

(takes a breath)

Getting carried away here! Anyway, it was a brilliant weekend and it's really inspired me! I know my mum really wants me to be a solicitor or something . . . but I think I want to be a writer!

(grins)

Sorry if this vlog is a bit boring or self-obsessed, but those of you who are readers or writers give us a thumbs-up in the comments below!

(puts on a cute baseball cap with: I ❤ books on it and salutes the camera)

Bye!

FADE OUT.

Views: 3,876

Subscribers: 9,135

Comments:

Sammylovesbooks: So envious. You got to meet John Green. ❤ Need to go next year.

lucylocket: So proud of you!

Amazing_Abby_xxx: Loved your outfit! Rocking it!

Thierryfromfrance: Congratulations! Watch out JK!

BookGeek: I've been to a different book conference called YALC – love hanging out with authors x

pink_sparkles: Must have been insane! So jel.

girlscanvlogfan: Next stop: SummerTube!

AlwaysFelicity: Hey, Hermione, I love to read too. Glad you're back with the gang :)

(scroll down to see 83 more comments)

Top Ten Tips for Making Your Own YouTube Videos

Here are some brilliant vlogging tips for those of you who are just getting started or who have been filming for a while like Hermione and the Girls Can Vlog gang.

Please remember that to set up a YouTube account you must be at least thirteen.

1) EXPERIMENT WITH SPECIALIST VIDEO EQUIPMENT

While many of you will be used to filming using your phones or digital cameras, you can get some great shots by using specialist video equipment.

A GoPro is a kind of digital camera, which is popular for filming extreme sports – such as skiing and snowboarding – and also for people who are travelling, as most of the models are so tiny they can fit in your pocket.

GoPros can be used on selfie-sticks or mounted to helmets, diving masks or on wrists so they can be used hands-free, as well as like a traditional camera.

All GoPros also have something called a fisheye lens – which means an extremely wide-angled lens – so you can capture a large group or a wide scene from up close. You can even use a GoPro underwater with a special waterproof casing.

2) TIPS FOR USING A GOPRO CAMERA

If you are lucky enough to be able to borrow or buy a GoPro or similar camera, here are some tips for filming from interesting or unusual angles:

Use a selfie-stick or mount to get great shots of yourself and your friends.

Set the frame rate at twenty-four to thirty frames per second for regular conditions and sixty or higher for slow-motion filming.

Get up close and personal when filming – the wide-angle lens means that, even up close, you will still capture a wide background scene.

Helmet mounts can result in shaky footage, but they do keep your hands free.

Experiment by strapping the GoPro to different things, such as the front of a snowboard, your dog's collar, or the paddle of your canoe!

3) MORE ADVANCED FILMING TIPS

Whether using a GoPro, a phone or a normal digital camera, there are loads of small things you can do to improve your film quality:

Always take extra batteries or a portable charging pack. Nothing is worse than running out of power when you're having fun. Batteries drain especially fast in cold conditions, so be wary of this if filming in the snow or underwater.

Shoot from as many different angles as you can so that when you come to edit your footage you'll have lots of various shots to choose from. Shooting from up high and down low, in front, behind and underneath things can make videos much more exciting.

But . . . be selective – or you will have tons of footage to sort through when editing.

Keep the lens of your camera clean! Dirt, water or snow can ruin a brilliant shot.

4) ADVANCED AUDIO

Have you ever filmed a brilliant video, only to discover that your microphone picked up too much background noise so the sound quality is terrible? Here's how you can improve your audio:

Try to film in quiet environments with limited background noise.

If you do need to film outdoors or in a noisy environment, use an external microphone rather than your camera or phone's built-in microphone. These don't have to be expensive, and you might be able to borrow one from your school.

The closer the microphone is to the speaker or sound source – the better.

Use a mono rather than a stereo microphone if possible to avoid picking up too much background noise.

5) MORE ADVANCED AUDIO TIPS

Another clever trick if you don't have a separate microphone to hand is to use the voice recording function on your phone to record sound, as opposed to using the audio track recorded by your digital camera.

This is especially useful if you're filming from a distance or you're aware that your shoot location is noisy.

Don't forget you will have to sync the audio track from your phone and the video track from your camera together later when editing. This can be done easily using even basic video-editing software.

6) ADVANCED EDITING

Editing can be great for cutting out mistakes you have

made during the video, but it can also be used to speed up your vlog. For example, removing silences and 'um's and 'ah's can keep your video punchy and keep your audience hooked.

Remember all those extra shots we were telling you to film earlier on? Well, cutting away to different shots and different scenes can be another way of keeping your viewers entertained. Don't be afraid to try new things, whether that be filming a portion of your video outside or even adding a funny skit in the middle.

Try out different transitions or even sound effects to make your video extra special.

7) WHAT IS TROLLING?

Trolling is a form of cyberbullying, in which a person or group of people use social media to bully another person. Trolling and cyberbullying are NEVER OK.

Even if the people responsible for the mean comments later say they were 'just joking' or that the person who is being bullied is 'taking things too seriously' – if someone makes a comment online that is deliberately designed to upset someone else, it is bullying.

8) HOW TO RESPOND TO NEGATIVE COMMENTS

The two essential points to remember if you are being bullied is that it is NOT YOUR FAULT and also that you NEED TO ASK FOR HELP.

Almost all YouTubers and other social-media users experience a form of cyberbullying at some point in their lives. Sadly, hiding behind the anonymity of cyberspace, people can be much meaner online than they ever would be in real life.

The best way to handle this is NOT to reply or get drawn into a dialogue. If you ignore them, cyberbullies will usually get bored and move on.

You can also delete hurtful comments and block the user. On YouTube you can also report the user by using the REPORT button or by going to www.youtube.com/reportabuse. You can report offensive comments on

Facebook, Instagram, Snapchat, WhatsApp and other social networks in the same way.

You can even blacklist particular words and phrases in your 'Community Settings' on YouTube and they will automatically go to your spam folder where you can approve them.

Make sure you tell a responsible adult, such as a parent, carer or teacher about any abuse you have encountered so they are able to support you.

9) WHAT IF THE BULLYING GETS WORSE?

If the abuse continues, or the comments are threatening and/or focusing on your sexual orientation, religion, race, disability or gender, you should take immediate action. These kinds of comments may be illegal and could result in the user making the comments being prosecuted by the police.

Before deleting the comment and blocking and reporting the user, take a screen grab of the comment as evidence in case the abuse requires further investigation.

Once again, make sure you get the support of a parent, carer, teacher or other responsible adult. Should the comment fall into the category of a hate crime or other threatening behaviour, they will be able to help you report it to the police.

10) REMEMBER . . . YOU ARE NOT ALONE

As well as telling a responsible adult, make sure you talk to your friends about what is happening so that they can help support you through this difficult experience. Many famous YouTubers have posted videos about how cyberbullying has affected them and how they have coped, and you may find these helpful.

There are also lots of charities that offer helplines and great advice about coping with and stopping bullying, for example:

* www.standuptobullying.co.uk
* www.bullying.co.uk
* www.ditchthelabel.org/get-help

Finally, always remember . . . **STAY SAFE ONLINE!** Ask your friends and family whether they are happy to be featured in videos BEFORE posting them. And NEVER EVER share your identity, address or the details of your school. Remember not to wear school uniform when filming, and be careful when vlogging in your garden if it's easily recognizable.

HAVE YOU READ . . .

AND COMING SOON!